THE WITCH OF DEMON ROCK

Also by Gabrielle Kent:

The Secrets of Hexbridge Castle
The Talisman Thief

THE WITCH OF DEMON ROCK

GABRIELLE KENT

SCHOLASTIC

Scholastic Children's Books
An imprint of Scholastic Ltd
Euston House, 24 Eversholt Street, London, NW1 1DB, UK
Registered office: Westfield Road, Southam, Warwickshire, CV47 0RA
SCHOLASTIC and associated logos are trademarks and/or
registered trademarks of Scholastic Inc.

First published in the UK by Scholastic Ltd, 2017

Copyright © Gabrielle Kent, 2017

The right of Gabrielle Kent to be identified as the author
of this work has been asserted by her.

ISBN 978 1407 15581 4

A CIP catalogue record for this book
is available from the British Library.

Printed by CPI Group (UK) Ltd, Croydon, CR0 4YY

Papers used by Scholastic Children's Books are made
from wood grown in sustainable forests.

1 3 5 7 9 10 8 6 4 2

This is a work of fiction. Names, characters, places, incidents and
dialogues are products of the author's imagination or are used
fictitiously. Any resemblance to actual people, living or
dead, events or locales is entirely coincidental.

www.scholastic.co.uk

For my dear friend Rhianna,
and all the staff at Hartlepool ARU.

From the bottom of my heart, thank you.

CONTENTS

PROLOGUE

Beneath the Yew Trees

June 1417

Newcastle

Few remembered the origin of the yew-topped hillock beyond the city walls. Those who did shuddered, crossed themselves and held their loved ones close whenever they passed by. On this cool midsummer night, a hooded man stood in the shadow of the yews. He knew what lay beneath the earth. It was why he had come.

Uncorking a bottle, he drew out a complex shape on the grass with a thick liquid that shone black in the moonlight. Sitting before it, he took a book from beneath his cloak and ran pale fingers over parchment that crackled with age. He began to chant – a low drone in a language older than the hills and darker than the beginning of time. A family of bats chittered out from the trees, chased by words that should never be spoken.

The chant repeated, over and over, curdling the night as something began to emerge from the earth – a black wisp of almost nothing, barely a shadow. It rose to hover over the symbol that stained the grass. The chant went on. More wisps rose from the earth like the blooming of a hellish garden.

Under the force of the chant they began to cling together, gaining in substance as a shrouded human form began to take shape – a wraith, as black as the shadows that formed it.

The chant stopped. The nearby forest held its breath.

Closing his book, the man rose and threw back his hood. The wraith rippled before him as if all the wisps were shivering at once.

"What am I to you?" he demanded of the wraith in a voice cold as death.

"Master," replied a hundred whispers.

"Yes." A smile crept across his thin lips. "Now

go. Search until you find that which was hidden. Find it. Take it. Bring it to me."

The wraith turned and glided down the hill; the grass touched by its tendrils shrivelled in its wake. As it disappeared into the forest the night was filled with the rustling of creatures fleeing from its path.

1

An Invitation

It was midnight on the first day of the summer holidays and Alfie Bloom was teaching Orin Hopcraft, the last of the great druids, the fine art of dunking biscuits into tea.

"You must give me the recipe for these," said Orin, brushing biscuit crumbs from his plaited beard. "What did you call these little chunks? Chocolate? It's marvellous, I must find some."

"You'll have to wait over a hundred years for it to reach England," said Alfie, pouring another cup of Earl Grey tea from the pot he had carried so carefully through the secret door into the druid's study before slipping six hundred years into the past. "I'll bring more next time I visit."

"I shall consider myself very lucky to have a supplier in the future," said Orin, as he popped the last chocolate chip into his mouth and slurped the rest of his tea. Alfie couldn't help but laugh at the sight of the druid drinking from a delicate floral teacup.

With the help of Ashford the butler, who Alfie had recently been astounded to discover was his own great-grandson, he had finally mastered his timeslip ability enough to travel to and from the past at will. Over the last month he had been visiting the 1400s twice a week to train with Orin. It hadn't exactly been as exciting as he had expected. Most of the time so far had been spent meditating and focussing his mind, something that the druid had insisted was one of the most important skills to learn.

"Right then," said Orin setting down his cup and saucer. "One last attempt at a trance state before you return home."

Alfie sighed and slipped from the footstool to sit cross-legged on the rug in front of the fire. He focussed on the candle the druid had placed on a small table between them and began to breathe deeply. Releasing the tension from every part of his body, just as Orin had taught him, Alfie let everything but the flickering flame slip away. When it finally felt as though the flame was all that existed, he closed his eyes and allowed himself to gently sink into a deep state of relaxation.

Breathing slowly, in and out, he felt a sort of shiver in the air around him. He opened his eyes – except he didn't. They were still closed, but it was as though he had woken up within his own trance. He was floating in the darkness as a shimmering silvery light flowed from his chest and swirled around him. He held out his hand and little sparks danced in the air where it brushed his fingertips

The light seemed almost playful as it darted around him. Alfie began to trace shapes in the air and the light flowed after his finger, copying them. Eventually he began to draw the shapes with just his thoughts – the light still traced each one perfectly, becoming more and more alive as Alfie tested it with more complex patterns. When he finally stopped, the light encircled him completely, forming a silver bubble in the centre of which Alfie floated, completely relaxed.

A tinkling sound broke gently through into Alfie's reverie and he allowed himself to float upwards. The silver light flowed back into his chest as he returned to consciousness. He opened his eyes. Orin put down the tiny silver bell he was ringing and clapped his hands.

"Excellent. Truly excellent! You reached a real trance state there. Your breathing was calm and controlled and I felt a wonderful sense of peace radiating out from you," Orin beamed. "Last month you couldn't sit quietly for five minutes. I'd never have thought this possible."

Alfie grinned. "Me neither. In the beginning, I couldn't stop thinking about other stuff, but now I can just let it all flow out of my mind." He remembered how bored and frustrated he had been in the first couple of weeks and how pointless he had thought the relaxation exercise. Now he actually enjoyed the sensation of slipping into the trance state. It had also made travelling between time periods so much easier.

"Something was different this time," said Alfie as he stood up and stretched his legs. He told Orin of the silvery light and the way he had interacted with it.

Orin chewed the last chocolate biscuit as he listened, thoughtfully. "And do you know what that light was?" he asked.

Alfie had wondered if it was just a dreamlike vision, but it had felt like more than that – like it was a part of him.

"It was the magic, wasn't it? The ancient magic you hid inside me the day I was born?"

Orin nodded. "I hadn't expected you to connect with it so quickly. It took me years. Perhaps the fact it has lived inside you for your whole life has made it more a part of you than it ever was of me. That connection with the magic will help greatly should anyone challenge you for it again. You must be able to control it, as it does not enjoy being suppressed. It wants to be used and will be drawn to those who would use it freely, despite the consequences."

"But that's not ever going to happen, is it?" said Alfie, warily. "Everyone that ever knew about it has gone. I'm safe, right?"

Orin's eyes flickered from Alfie to the crackling fire. "If time has taught us anything, it's that nothing can be assumed."

The hairs on Alfie's arms prickled as he thought of the danger his inheritance had brought to him and his friends and family and tried to shake off the fear that was creeping over him. "If I'm going to be challenged for my magic, I'll need to be able to defend myself. So, what can you teach me?"

Orin smiled. "I know you found this dull at first, but being able to control your mind is vital for the things I need to teach you if you are to be my apprentice. There is much for you to learn: potions, herbology, spells. All of this will help you to protect yourself, and your friends. It will involve some travelling. You will need to spend some longer periods of time here. Perhaps a week or two to start with."

"You mean come and stay in the past?" Alfie's eyes lit up. In all his recent visits to the 1400s, he had not ventured beyond Orin's study. The thought of exploring fifteenth-century Hexbridge filled him with excitement. He bit his lip as he suddenly thought of his cousins, Madeleine and Robin, and his best friend, Amy Siu. They had so many plans for adventures during the summer holidays.

"Could my cousins and Amy come and stay too?" he asked. "You've already met Robin when he got dragged back in time with me, and they all know about you. Please?"

Orin scratched his cheek. "Hmm, they have already proven worthy compatriots. It may do them good to learn some of what I am to teach you."

"Is that a yes?" said Alfie, tensing for the druid's answer.

"They would be most welcome here," said Orin. Alfie punched both fists up into the air. "But! We need to arrange this properly. I think it's high time I was reintroduced to your father."

"You realize that if you're messing with us, I'll *have* to kill you," said Amy, who was brandishing a jam spoon in a manner that had Alfie fully believing she could do real damage with it. They were sitting in Hexbridge's newest café – a Victorian tearoom jointly run by Lizzie Tiptree, Amy's gran, and Gertie Entwhistle, the town's baker and sweetshop owner.

"No joke," said Alfie, staving off the spoon with his butter-knife as Madeleine and Robin clapped their hands. "Orin invited me to stay for two weeks, and he said you could all come too."

"Weapons down!" said a small woman in a Victorian maid's uniform and white trainers as she passed by holding a gigantic chocolate cake.

"Ceasing hostilities, Gran," said Amy, sticking the spoon back in the blackcurrant jam and holding up her hands. The four friends beamed at each other over a cake stand loaded with sandwiches and sweet treats.

"So what's Orin going to teach you?" asked Robin.

Alfie shrugged. "Part of being his apprentice is learning herbs, potions and spells. He's going to teach me how to use them for protection."

"After everything that's happened since you moved here, that's probably a good idea," said Robin.

"You should ask him to teach you how to create things with your magic, like Ashford can!" said Madeleine. "You'll be able to make anything you want, like a canoe … or a wooden fort … or a target range for archery practice!"

"Um, aren't those all things that you want, Madds?" said Amy, giving her a nudge.

"I don't think I'll be doing any of that," said Alfie. "I wouldn't want to either." He shuddered. On the few occasions it revealed itself, the magic had more control over him than he had over it. Orin was right: it was too dangerous to use.

"The old druids were philosophers, herbalists, teachers, poets, astronomers, magicians…" said Robin, his eyes shining. "Just think of everything he could teach you, all of that ancient knowledge you could bring back to the world!"

"Sounds like you want those lessons more than Alfie," said Madeleine.

Amy drummed her fingers on the table. "So when are we going?"

"Yes!" said Madeleine. "There's so much to pack! I'll need my bow and arrows, my penknife, fishing hooks, walking boots. . ."

"I don't know about the boots," said Amy. "Won't we need to dress like we're from Orin's time? You don't want to get burnt as a witch for wearing future clothes!"

"They didn't do that in Orin's time, did they?" gaped Madeleine.

"Actually, the witch hunts started in Europe in around 1450. . ." began Robin.

"Hold your horses!" said Alfie. "Before you go packing and worrying about that stuff, this whole thing depends on whether or not Dad's OK with it. Orin wants to meet him tomorrow morning, and it's going to be difficult enough for Dad to get his head around the fact that I can timeslip."

"Uncle Will's cool," said Robin. "I'm sure he'll say yes, won't he?"

Alfie didn't answer, but under the table he crossed his fingers, tightly.

2

The Conditions

July 1417

Northumberland

Deep in the woods, in the moonlight shadows, an owl hooted a warning and retreated into its nest. A doe raised its head and sniffed. A red squirrel paused in its foraging and pricked up its ears. Faint whispers began to creep between the trees. Something was coming.

The squirrel shot up into its drey and curled its tail around its young. The doe bolted, crashing through the undergrowth. Even spiders scuttled for cover and huddled under leaves. Soon the woods were silent but for the sorrowful whispers that filled the air.

The wraith floated into the clearing – a shadow as dark as a hole torn in the night. It paused and hovered, trailing wisps of darkness. It had no eyes with which to see, but it scented the air, searching. It did not know its destination, it was as if it didn't even exist, but if it was to return to the cool embrace of the earth it must find what its master was looking for. A nearby village drew its attention from its search... *Life*, whispered its many voices longingly. It drifted silently from the clearing. As it departed the entire wood breathed a sigh of relief.

The wraith headed towards the peaceful town. Plants wilted at its touch as it floated through a herb garden towards a small cottage on the outskirts of the village. Voices and laughter came from within. A family. The wraith remembered family. It stopped at the threshold and raised arms of shifting shadows, feeling vibrations in the air. There had been magic here, but simple folk magic, not the ancient power that it sought. It turned to leave, but the warmth and joy within the cottage pulled it back. *Life,* its voices whispered again. Unable to resist its hunger, the wraith floated through the cottage door.

When it finally left, it raised a long, black finger

and traced a shape on the outside of the front door, a shape that each of the souls trapped within the wraith recognized. A little less cold and afraid, the wraith glided away, retreating into the night.

In the cottage with the black cross upon the door, the laughter had stopped.

The next morning saw Alfie's dad sitting nervously in one of the armchairs by the fire in the castle library, a letter clutched in his hand.

"So what do we do now?" he asked Alfie.

The letter had been delivered by a raven from Muninn and Bone solicitors the previous afternoon. The bird had nearly caused an explosion as it flew in through the workshop window and dropped the letter into the workings of a rather unstable miniature generator that Alfie's dad was currently working on. The letter read:

Muninn and Bone Solicitors (Est. 1086)

Dear Mr William Horatio Bloom,

Our client, Orin Hopcraft, has requested to meet with you at 10 a.m. on Tuesday 25th July, 1417, to discuss the commencement of Master Alfie Bloom's training.

The meeting will take place in the castle library. Your journey to the fifteenth century will be facilitated by your son.

Regards,
Caspian Bone
Partner

Alfie had suggested the library as the venue for the meeting and was glad that Orin had agreed. He wanted to keep the druid's study a secret shared only with the twins and Amy, and was a little worried that his dad might claim the study for himself if he ever saw the shelves full of amazing handwritten tomes and weird and wonderful objects.

A loud chirp alerted him to another of the castle's weird and wonderful objects as it watched them from its perch on the head of one of the Fates above the fireplace, Leonardo da Vinci's silver sparrow. They had found it in what Alfie had named the Treasure Room in the eastern tower. Ever since the elf queen had passed some of her magic into it, it almost seemed as if it was truly alive. Alfie was quite glad that it had taken a liking to his dad as he found it rather annoying himself.

17

He had named it Sparky because it seemed to have a spark of real life since its encounter with the elf queen.

"Are you ready to go, Dad?" asked Alfie.

"Yes, but I still don't understand. How can we possibly travel to 1417 to meet Orin Hopcraft?"

Alfie took a deep breath and sat on the little table next to his dad's chair. "OK, Dad. Remember the night I was born? You told me that you somehow slipped back in time six hundred years to when Orin lived here."

"How could I forget?" said his dad. "It seemed like a crazy dream your mother and I had shared, until the day that strange solicitor Caspian Bone told us that Orin had left you the castle."

"Well … when Caspian told us we were getting the castle before my thirteenth birthday, he mentioned that it was because he had seen me timeslip."

Alfie's dad's mouth dropped open. "You timeslipped? How is that possible?" Before Alfie could even answer his dad slapped his own forehead with his palm and continued, "Well, of course it is possible! You were born six hundred years in the past, so you belong there as much as here. It makes absolute sense that you are a part of both time periods. Tell me, does time keep ticking here when you visit the past? I imagine it must as you are living a single lifetime across two time periods. . ."

Alfie listened to his dad conducting a conversation with himself and could hardly believe how quickly he seemed to have got his head around the idea of his son being a time traveller. He was already way past amazement and into theorizing on the nature of time travel.

"So, how many times have you travelled into the past? Have you already met Orin?"

"We'd better get a move on, Dad," said Alfie quickly. "We don't want to be late." He didn't really want to let his dad know that the first couple of times he had timeslipped had been near-death experiences, or that he had already started sneaking off to the past to train with the druid.

"OK then, how does this work?"

"As long as you are holding on to me when I timeslip, you'll travel with me. Probably best if you close your eyes." The one time Alfie had tried slipping through time with his eyes open had left him disorientated for days. Closing his own eyes, he hooked his arm through his dad's and held on tight. He soon felt the familiar tugging sensation in his chest and let it drag him back in time, back to the time period that was his second home.

"We're here, Dad," he said, unhooking his arm after several dizzying seconds. They were still in the castle library, which looked very much the same as it did in the present day with one exception. Orin Hopcraft was sitting opposite them, a wide grin on his face.

"Mr Bloom," he said, reaching out and shaking Alfie's dad's hand vigorously. "So good to see you again."

Alfie's dad's jaw worked up and down uselessly until he finally managed to stammer, "Likewise." He looked around the library. "So, we're … um … we're really in the past?"

"Well, it's very much the present for me," said Orin. "But yes, it is a pleasure to welcome you back, nearly thirteen years after your last visit." He led Alfie and his dad to the window, through which they could see a very different Hexbridge with fewer houses and many more trees.

"Alfie," said the druid gently. "Your father and I have much to catch up on and discuss. Would you mind if we talk alone? I'm sure he'd also like a tour of the castle before he leaves."

Alfie glanced at his dad, who looked as though

he was trying to resist the urge to run straight down to the village to explore medieval rural England.

"OK," said Alfie, a little reluctantly as he wondered whether there was something the druid didn't want him to hear. "But don't show him any machinery, or he'll be here all day taking it apart and putting it back together again."

"That's enough cheek," said his dad, giving him a nudge. "Off you pop now. I'm sure Amy and the twins are already getting impatient."

Alfie found the twins and Amy waiting in his bedroom when he slipped back into his own time.

"So? What did Uncle Will say?" asked Madeleine.

"Give him a chance, he's only just got there!" said Alfie, flopping down with the others on his gigantic bed. "He'll be back some time after lunch."

"Gah!" exploded Madeleine, throwing herself back on to the pillows. "You could have at least taken us with you."

"Be patient, Maddie," said Robin. "If Uncle Will says yes we'll get to spend lots of time there."

"That's all right for you to say," huffed Madeleine. "You've already been to the past with Alfie, AND you met Orin!"

Alfie's mind flashed back to the time he had hit

his head in the caves under the Hexbridge hills and had accidentally dragged Robin back in time with him as he fell unconscious. They had met Orin's friend, Bryn the woodsman, who had bandaged Alfie's wounds and helped them get home.

"That's not fair, Maddie. It wasn't exactly fun for Robin."

"Really? Then how come he didn't stop talking about it for months!"

"Enough!" said Amy, clapping her hands over her ears. "You're all giving me a headache. Come on, let's see what Ash is up to."

Ashford was weeding the herb garden and putting in some new plants. He was fully recovered from his injuries after being shot with an arrow and kidnapped by elves only a couple of months before. Alfie felt a little odd about having his own descendant working for him, but Ashford seemed perfectly happy with the arrangement, especially as it meant avoiding alternate punishment for his previous life as the greatest thief the world had ever seen.

They joined him in weeding, turning the soil, digging up vegetables and pruning overgrown plants.

"Have you spoken to Emily recently, Ashford?"

asked Alfie as he pulled up a bunch of carrots and brushed off the soil.

"Yeah," grinned Amy, slyly. "Has she picked a wedding dress yet?"

"Emily is quite well, thank you," said Ashford. "But she's helping her mother stabilize the elven realms, so the wedding may have to wait quite a while."

Madeleine snorted so suddenly that everyone turned to stare at her.

"I've just thought," she giggled. "Emily's mum, the elf queen that nearly wrecked Alfie's castle – she's going to be your mother-in-law!"

Ashford sighed and got back to digging. "Don't think I haven't thought about that!"

Alfie's dad didn't return from the past until around three o'clock, at which point everyone was in the kitchen helping Ashford chop vegetables, hang herbs, and make chutneys out of multi-coloured tomatoes picked from the new greenhouse. He materialized in the kitchen with a pop that made Alfie squeeze the tomato he was skinning so hard that it exploded, showering everyone with juice and seeds.

"Excellent, you're all here!" Alfie thought his dad seemed almost as surprised to see them as they were at his sudden appearance. "What an experience. Time travel! I mean, what inventor *hasn't* thought of creating a time machine? But to really experience it ... well, I think I could use a nice strong cup of tea!"

Ashford fixed a tray of tea and biscuits, which they shared in the Abernathy Room as Alfie's dad shared details of his trip to medieval Hexbridge.

"... and from the eastern tower I could see a watermill down on the river before it meets Archelon Lake. All that's there today is an outline in the grass – how amazing to be able to see what had been there with my own eyes! And then there's the village itself, did you know—"

"Dad!" said Alfie, trying not to shout despite his impatience. "That's all very interesting, but what did *Orin* say? Did he ask you about us visiting him for a couple of weeks?"

"Yes, he did."

"Well...?"

"It would be the longest you've ever been away from home, Alfie."

"I know, but I'd still be at home, just in a different time, and we can come back if we do get homesick."

"Which we won't!" added Amy.

"So, can we go?" asked Alfie.

"I know you were born there, but the time period will still be very strange to you. There may be lots of dangers I haven't even thought about." He scratched his head. "But Orin Hopcraft is so intelligent... I'm sure he's thought of everything..."

"DAD!" Alfie pounded the frayed arm of the sofa so hard that he ended up choking on a cloud of dust. "Yes or no?" he coughed.

"Yes, I suppose..."

Alfie, the twins and Amy leapt up on to the sofa for a group hug, bouncing up and down as the springs begged for mercy.

"On one condition."

Alfie's head whipped round as he wondered what sort of terrible rule his dad was going to impose.

"I need to file some important patents over the next few weeks, and I don't want you all going alone."

Alfie groaned. Was his dad going to make him wait weeks? If they didn't go soon they wouldn't be able to go at all once school started in September.

"So ... I propose that Ashford goes with you."

Alfie looked to the butler, who nearly dropped

the teapot he was holding.

"Ashford, you came to us from Muninn and Bone, so I imagine you know more about Alfie's ability to timeslip than I did. And you kept him safe when the castle was invaded by those elves."

Alfie noticed Ashford cast him a guilty glance. His dad didn't know that it was actually Alfie, the twins and Amy who kept the wounded Ashford safe during the siege.

"Well, if they want me to come. . ."

"Of course we do!" said Alfie.

"I've never been so far back in time. This will be my first meeting with Orin. Chronologically, anyway."

"So you've met him before?" asked Alfie, wondering just how many secrets the butler still had to share.

Ashford winked and instead answered, "I'd be delighted to travel with you!"

Alfie threw his arms around his dad's shoulders and gave him a big squeeze before leaping down from the sofa to high five the butler.

"Right then," grinned Amy. "When do we leave?"

*

Two days later, Alfie lay in bed wide-awake with

excitement as the birds outside chirped and twittered through their dawn chorus – he had hardly slept a wink. He couldn't stop thinking about the trip he would be making to the past in a few hours. His bag was already sitting on his desk, ready to go. He had packed light as Orin was going to supply them with appropriate clothing, although Robin had instructed everyone to bring plenty of underwear, saying:

"I'm not sure what pants were made out of in medieval times, but I'll bet it wasn't comfortable!"

Alfie groaned as he realized he'd forgotten to pack shampoo. He jumped out of bed and instantly regretted it as the rug flew out from under his feet, sending him crashing to the floor.

"What's happening? Is it morning yet? Are we going now?" boomed a deep voice. "I'd *bear*-ly gotten to sleep!"

"Artan! Shhh!" groaned Alfie, getting up and rubbing his bruised bottom. "It's only five o'clock." He had forgotten that the bearskin rug had spent the night sleeping next to his bed, ready to leave for Orin's time with them. At least the shock had reminded Alfie of what he had forgotten to pack. He limped to the panel by his wardrobe and pushed the knot in the wood that opened the secret door to his own bathroom. Grabbing the shampoo, he zipped it inside one of the pockets in his bag then climbed back into his four-poster bed as Artan settled again on the floor.

The second Alfie closed his eyes there was a sharp tapping at the window. He sighed and threw back the covers, giving up on ever getting back to sleep as he stomped over to the window. Flinging open the curtains, he blinked against the light morning sky.

A large raven was sitting on the window ledge, wings neatly folded to its sides as it rapped the glass impatiently with its beak. It wasn't the first time Alfie had been woken by one of Caspian Bone's messengers. He opened the window and held out his hand.

"OK, give me the note, and tell Caspian to stop sending messages in the middle of the night!"

The raven ignored his hand and hopped in through the open window, beak held high. There was a rustling of feathers, and Alfie leapt back off the window seat as the bird began to change shape. Artan floated beside Alfie, growling as the raven stretched and shimmered before them, wings folding neatly into arms, talons turning to shiny black shoes. Its beak shrunk back into a paling face, until finally a tall man was sitting on the window seat brushing the lapels of his immaculate Victorian-style suit.

"Good morning," said Caspian Bone.

Alfie blushed bright red as he realized he had been complaining to the solicitor himself.

"I apologize if I disturbed you."

"That's fine," mumbled Alfie. "I was already awake."

"Artan," said Caspian, nodding curtly to the floating bearskin rug.

"Caspian," replied the bear, bobbing slightly.

The solicitor glanced around the room, taking in the packed bag on the dresser. "I see you are prepared for your trip."

"Yes," said Alfie, suddenly worried. "It's still happening, isn't it? Orin hasn't sent a message to say we can't go?"

"*You* will still be travelling back in time," said Caspian. "However, I have been made aware that you intend to take the bear and the butler with you."

Alfie didn't even bother asking how he knew. The ravens stationed on the walls took word of anything that happened at Hexbridge Castle straight to Muninn and Bone.

"We have given Ashford our permission to

travel with you. However, Artan *must* remain here."

"WHAT!" exploded Artan, swooping around the room leaving papers and comics spiralling in his wake. "How dare you fly in here and tell Alfie what I can and can't do, as if I wasn't even here!"

"Calm yourself," snapped Caspian. "Alfie, may we discuss this in private?"

Alfie caught the bear's paw as he whizzed past and dragged him to a stop.

"If it involves Artan, then he should be here to hear it," said Alfie, stroking the bear's fur to calm him down. "He was Orin's friend, so why can't he come back with me to visit him?"

"That is exactly the problem. In 1417 Orin is *not* Artan's friend. The bear does not exist in his current form in that time."

"So what does that matter?" asked Alfie. "I can introduce them."

Caspian sighed, but before he could explain, Artan gently placed his paw on Alfie's shoulder.

"Much as I hate to admit it," he rumbled, "the bird is right. Orin created me when my life as a bear was taken early. I don't remember much about that, but if I meet Orin before I am supposed to, well ... it might change things."

"But Ashford can't travel back in time that

far himself. So *he'll* be meeting Orin before he's supposed to. Why can't you?"

Artan shook his shaggy head. "If the bird says I shouldn't go, then it is probably for good reason."

Alfie took some comfort in seeing Caspian bristle at being referred to as a bird for the second time.

"Then it is agreed," said Caspian, climbing on to the window ledge and looking back at Alfie. "Artan remains here."

With that he leapt from the ledge. A second later a large black raven soared up and off into the dawn.

3

Orin's Castle

At noon, Alfie, the twins, and Amy Siu stood together in the courtyard, bags packed. Alfie had decided they should enter the castle through the front door like real visitors, rather than just arriving inside Orin's study. The twins had their bows and quivers strung across their backs and Alfie had packed five big bars of chocolate and a tin of cocoa for the druid.

Alfie's dad had concocted a story about a summer history camp for the twins' parents and Amy's gran.

"It wasn't exactly a lie," he said guiltily. "You will be learning an awful lot about medieval times, first-hand!"

The twins' parents were quite happy to send them on a free educational trip and Amy's gran had agreed as soon as she heard that there wouldn't be any computers or phones.

"It'll do you the world of good to get away from screens for a while," she had told Amy two days ago. "Just make sure you write to me three times a week."

"Ugh, writing! With a pen? On paper? Like some kind of caveman?"

"She will." Alfie had jumped in before Amy went too far and risked changing her gran's mind. Muninn and Bone had delivered a number of letters from the past to him, all at times set by the druid. So he assumed it wouldn't be too difficult to arrange to send letters home.

"I still don't understand why Artan can't come," said Madeleine, looking up to Artan's tower. Guilt ran through Alfie's chest as he wondered if the bear was watching them, nose pressed up against his window.

"Probably a time paradox," said Robin, as he struggled to squeeze a compass and a map of Northumberland into his bulging rucksack.

"*You're* a time paradox," said Madeleine, holding the bag closed for him as he zipped it shut.

"Come to see us off, Leo?" Alfie called to the ginger tomcat as he slunk across the courtyard to rub himself against everyone's legs.

"Galileo won't even notice we've gone," laughed Amy as the cat rolled over in a patch of sunlight and swiped at a butterfly flying too close for safety.

Ashford emerged from the kitchens. "Ready to go?" he asked. He had a hessian potato sack strapped across his back. "My suitcase," he grinned as he saw Alfie staring at it. "Thought it seemed more authentic than your backpacks."

Alfie's dad came hurrying out of the castle doors with a first-aid kit and a bundle of notebooks, which he stuffed into Alfie's bag. "Orin knows a lot about healing, but I'm sure there weren't any waterproof plasters in medieval times, so take this with you. The notebooks are for you to write down everything Orin teaches you. Make sure you take your studies seriously – this is an amazing opportunity for you all.

His eyes misted over as he seemed to disappear into a daydream where he was studying with Orin himself.

"We'd better be off, Orin's waiting," said Alfie quickly, before his dad decided to come with them.

"Yes, of course." Alfie's dad gave him a quick

hug, as though not trusting himself to let go if he held on any longer. "Enjoy yourself, Alfie, and I'll see you soon."

"Ready?" Alfie asked the others. They all nodded, picked up their bags and huddled together in a rugby scrum, eyes closed as they all held on to Alfie's arms. Even with four people clinging to him, it didn't take much effort for Alfie to focus and send them all whooshing through time. He was quite proud of how easily he could do this now. With a pop, they were suddenly right back where they started, but in 1417.

"It's the same . . . but different," cried Madeleine, dropping her bags and dashing around the courtyard. It looked a little wilder than in Alfie's time, but just as beautiful. The vegetable and herb gardens were much larger, and several scrawny chickens were pecking around in the soil under the apple trees. On the grass a cow and several sheep were grazing while two spotted pigs gobbled from a trough.

"They're so small!" said Alfie, marvelling at the animals. They looked very different to the animals on his aunt and uncle's farm. "Has Orin done something to them?"

"That's how they were back then. I mean,

back … now," said Robin. "Before they were bred to become larger for more meat."

"Oi, get out of my pockets!" shouted Amy. Alfie laughed to see her wrestling her jacket out of the mouth of a goat. There was a tearing noise and the goat bounded off across the courtyard with half of Amy's pocket and a white paper bag. "Bring back those macaroons!" she yelled. Before she could give chase, the great wooden doors to the castle swung open and Orin Hopcraft stood before them, arms wide.

"Welcome to Hexbridge Castle," he beamed, and then glanced at Amy's torn pocket. "Oh dear, I see you've already met Wesley."

Alfie could see everyone's eyes darting into every corner as they entered the castle where he introduced them all to Orin. Ashford seemed the most excited to meet the druid. His eyes shone as he pumped his hand up and down.

"I can't believe it!" he kept saying. "It must be eighty years until the first time I meet you, and you look exactly the same. Maybe a little less grey, but that's all!"

"Well, I'm very glad to hear I'll still have hair to go grey," laughed the druid. "But please, no talk of my future – it is not set in stone. Time is a delicate thing and the more we play with it, the more likely we are to cause ripples that become waves. Best not to know a future that might not come about. Now, I imagine you'd like a tour?"

The first stop was the eastern tower, which Alfie had only discovered the entrance to only a couple of months earlier

"If you please, Alfie," said Orin, indicating the stone carving of the two knights that guarded the entrance. Alfie pressed the four bricks that caused the carving to slide aside, revealing the entrance to the tower.

Alfie noticed there was very little stored in it as they hurried up the spiral staircase to the top. No wonderful costumes from around the world, no strange and incredible treasures gifted to the druid for services he had rendered to some of the most interesting, talented and powerful people in the medieval world. Orin obviously hadn't travelled far beyond England's shores yet. Alfie guessed that would change when the druid met Artan. He wondered when and why Leonardo da Vinci would give Sparky, the little silver clockwork sparrow, to the druid. He was glad that his dad had the bird to keep him company, along with Galileo, while they were away.

Everyone stood silent as they reached the top of the tower. Alfie could see all the way out to the sea, some thirty miles away. He had seen the magnificent view of Hexbridge and the surrounding area before, but as well as the larger forest and smaller plots of farmed land, even the air in this century seemed different.

"Smell that air!" said Ashford, taking a lungful.

Alfie sniffed; he could faintly smell woodsmoke and manure, but underneath all of that was a freshness he wasn't used to. He had felt much better since moving from the city to Hexbridge, but the clean air here made him feel almost dizzy as he sucked it in.

"So much wild land, all these trees, and no cars," said Ashford, gazing wistfully across the landscape.

"There are hardly any houses," said Alfie. "How many people are there in England right now?"

"Around two-and-a-half million," Robin answered immediately. Alfie smiled. His cousin had read everything he could on the fifteenth century over the last two days.

"You study your books well," said Orin. "Now, on with the tour, although I'll leave some places for you to discover on your own. It's more fun that way, don't you think?"

The layout of Orin's castle wasn't so different from Alfie's. Obviously the quirky modern improvements that had been carried out for Alfie and his dad hadn't happened yet, but it wasn't draughty and dark as he had expected a medieval castle to be. The corridors were light due to the large leaded windows, and in the darker rooms Orin clapped his hands and the torches on the walls burst into flame.

"Nice," said Amy, nodding approvingly.

The main difference Alfie noticed was the southern tower. It didn't exist. Alfie had spotted that the tower was missing when they had arrived in the courtyard, although he still checked under a tapestry for the door as they passed the spot where it existed in his castle.

"Maybe he built it just for Art—" Robin clamped his hand over his sister's mouth before she finished saying the bear's name.

"What was that?" asked Orin as they headed back down to the ground floor.

"Maddie was just admiring all of the ... art!" said Robin quickly.

"I do like to collect tapestries and curios," said Orin with a smile. "I wish I had time to travel more. I'd love to visit far-off lands, perhaps travel to Italy and see some of the great masters at work." Alfie noticed the druid's eyes mist over with thoughts of Renaissance Italy as they headed downstairs.

"And he will, when he meets Artan," whispered Madeleine. "What!" she demanded as Robin tried to hush her again. "I'M WHISPERING!"

The next stop was the cellars. Passing through the undercroft, which served as a pantry in the future, Alfie could see that it had much the same use here.

"So that's what those hooks are for," said Ashford, pointing to the pheasants, rabbits and strips of dried meat hanging from the ceiling.

"Ah yes," said Orin. "Bryn brings me more than I can possibly eat. I give much of it to the villagers."

"Bryn!" said Alfie, beaming as he remembered it as the name of the man who had helped him and Robin when he had slipped through time deep in the caves under Hexbridge Hill.

"Will we see him?" he hoped so, he couldn't remember if he had thanked him properly and looked forward to meeting the jovial woodsman again.

"Of course," said Orin. "In fact he'll be here for supper tonight."

Madeleine cheered. "Robin told me all about him," she told Amy. "He sounds really interesting!"

Ashford was rubbing his chin as he contemplated the meat.

"I thought that it was illegal for anyone to hunt in the king's forests?"

"Yes, most of the forests in Britain were – are reserved for the king and nobles to go hunting," said Robin, unable to stop himself from sharing information.

"The kings of England and I have always had an understanding," said Orin. "It serves them well to have a druid in their kingdom, and they have granted me lordship of Hexbridge, which includes the forest. Everyone in Hexbridge owns their own land and can forage freely for food in my forest without fear of execution."

"Whoa," said Amy as Orin handed out torches and led the way deeper into the cellars. "Punishment in medieval time is *harsh*!"

Alfie made up his mind to stay well within the confines of Hexbridge during his visit.

Orin led the way straight down to the lower cellars. Their torches sent long shadows flickering behind them as they descended and worked their way through the maze of chambers.

"I've always wondered about this room," said Alfie, as they passed through the room containing the deep pool that connected to Archelon Lake. "The castle already seems to be drawing water from somewhere, so why do you need this well?" Alfie had travelled out into the lake twice via the pool – both times had almost ended in disaster. This was why, in Alfie's own castle, his dad had covered it with a heavy wooden lid.

The druid stirred the water gently with his finger and the torchlight glinted in the ripples in the black water. "A dark, still pool is very useful for magic. This one only ever sees the light that we bring into the cellars, which makes it perfect for scrying."

"Scrying? You mean seeing things that are happening, like in your black mirror?" asked Alfie, remembering the strange mirror Amy had found in Artan's room, which let them see into different rooms in the castle.

"You've found that?" said Orin, grinning widely. "Yes, it is a very useful tool. But I use this pool to try to see further, sometimes even through time. Though it's the one skill that I struggle to master. The only time I have successfully seen through time was when I was preparing to pass the ancient creation magic on to you as the Fates had decreed, and I think they may have had a hand in that."

"What about the seal?" asked Robin, as Orin started to lead them back the way they came.

"Yes," said Alfie, glad that Robin had asked. "Aren't you going to tell us anything about it?"

Alfie knew that the great sealed trapdoor in the deepest, darkest corner of the cellars marked the entrance to where the last of the dragons slept deep underground. Ashford had been knocked unconscious in these very cellars as the two of them had tried to stop Alfie's evil headmistresses' attempt to waken the dragons. He felt Ashford squeeze his shoulder and knew that the butler still felt guilty for not being able to protect Alfie.

Orin paused. "There is still much to tell you about the seal, Alfie. It is quite safe as long as it remains in place, but there are things you must know and things I must teach you. Forgive me, but I wish to leave that for a later time."

Alfie wondered what more there was to learn about the seal as the druid led them back through the cellars. They stopped briefly in the well-stocked undercroft.

"Could you help me carry some of this upstairs?" asked Orin. Alfie grabbed several small loaves of bread while the twins and Amy loaded themselves up with cheeses wrapped in leafy herbs, pickled vegetables and a large stoneware jug of milk. Ashford picked up a tray of delicious-looking pies. Alfie's stomach began to growl as he wondered what was under the buttery glazed crust.

"Ho, Orin!" boomed a deep voice as they climbed the steps to the kitchen. "Have your guests arrived yet?"

"See for yourself," said the druid, sweeping aside as Alfie and the others poured into the kitchen behind him.

"Bryn!" shouted Alfie at the sight of the tall, bearded man stirring the contents of a large pot over the kitchen fire. Bryn beamed with delight to see them and wiped his hands on the shaggy sheepskin waistcoat he wore over his tunic.

"Great to see you again, lads!" he bellowed, clapping Alfie and Robin on their backs so hard that Alfie thought his stomach was going to fly out of his mouth. Seeing Madeleine and Amy, Bryn bowed deeply and tried unsuccessfully to adopt a more genteel tone.

"And a pleasure to make yer acquaintance, lasses!"

Alfie laughed as both girls awkwardly attempted curtsies in response to Bryn's fairly formal greeting. They gave up trying to figure out what to do with their legs and shook Bryn's great calloused hands instead. The woodsman looked at their jeans and T-shirts and shook his head, a great big grin spreading across his face.

"Well, I'd hardly believe it. Orin told me you're all from six hundred years hence, but I didn't figure there would ever be a day when lads and lasses would start dressing the same! Tell me, do men wear bodices in the future?"

He continued to chuckle to himself as he lifted the pot from the stove and grabbed some wooden bowls.

"Right then. Take that lot into the Great Hall. We're having a right big feast of a supper tonight!"

It certainly was a feast. By the time they sat down at the table it contained a whole assortment of pies, fruit, bread, pickles and cheeses. Bryn ladled out an oaty stew from the pot he had brought with him.

"This is really good. What's in it?" asked Alfie, swirling the mix with his spoon.

"That's my own pottage recipe," said Bryn. "What isn't in it! Oatmeal, thyme, sweet marjoram, parsley, chives, marigolds, strawberry and violet leaves, beets, borage, sorrel, sage, salt and a good hunk of mutton. Caught the boar and rabbits for the pies myself, too. They're my wife's recipe."

Alfie had eaten rabbit pie cooked by his Aunt Grace, but he had never tried boar before. It was dark meat, a bit like beef, and Bryn had added forest mushrooms to the filling. As he bit through the pastry and into the rich, juicy filling, Alfie felt his taste buds give a little cheer.

"Bryn practically keeps Hexbridge running," said Orin. "He cuts wood and ploughs for those that can't, feeds the hungry and keeps the woods safe. There isn't a wolf or boar that would attack a fly while he patrols the forest."

"What about bears – are there many still around?" asked Madeleine, cutting the last pie in half and giving the biggest piece to Amy. She stifled a little yelp and Alfie guessed that Robin had clipped her ankle with his foot for getting too close to mentioning Artan again.

"Bears?" laughed Bryn. "Now bears you don't need to worry about. Never exactly seen one myself. Extinct, some will tell you."

"Time for a special toast," said Orin.

The druid poured everyone a cup of juice that

smelt of sweet berries and mint, and then took a small bottle from the pouch on his belt.

"Robin, on your last visit to the past, do you remember how you returned home?"

"It was easy," said Robin. "I really wanted to get back to find Maddie. As soon as I recognized the marker stone outside our farm it was like I just appeared back home."

Orin rested his elbows on the table. "That was because you don't belong in this time. Alfie was born here and can stay as long as he wishes. However, you three," he indicated Amy and the twins, "may well be pulled home at any time you think of it fondly. Even Ashford runs that risk, as he cannot travel this far back himself. Without Alfie, you would be unable to rejoin us should you take an unexpected trip home. That is why I have brewed this."

He held up the bottle. Alfie was mesmerized by the shimmering light radiating from it like a blue beacon in the Great Hall, which was lit only with candles and flickering torches.

"A few drops of this potion will anchor you to the past for over a week, after which you may have recovered from any initial homesickness which could drag you through time. There are no side effects other than it becoming more difficult for you to return home over the next seven days. Now..." He looked from the twins to Amy and Ashford. "It's up to you whether or not you take the potion."

Four cups immediately appeared under his nose.

"There's no way I'm getting dragged back home," said Amy. "Gran will have me washing up in the café while you lot have all the fun!"

Orin carefully measured out several drops of potion into the brew in each cup. Alfie watched everyone's drinks turn a slightly shimmering purple. He wondered if Orin would expect him to learn to brew potions. He had helped Orin mix several but couldn't remember all of the steps. How would he ever learn the magical language that the druid spoke over his potions when he was having enough trouble with Mrs Salvador's Spanish class?

When he had finished measuring out the potion, Orin held his own cup high and announced:

"To life, loyalty, and learning!"

"Life, loyalty, and learning!" everyone chanted, knocking their glasses together and downing the potion.

Orin rubbed his hands together. "Right then. As

lessons will start tomorrow, I'd like to hear about school in your time."

Alfie wasn't at all surprised that Robin took the lead in the conversation, filling Orin in on all of the subjects they were taking at Wyrmwald House. Orin was particularly interested in science and art lessons in the future. He avoided talking too much about what they studied in history class. Alfie was hardly surprised after what he had said about the risks of knowing too much about the future.

Before they knew it, the fire had burnt low and everyone was yawning over their empty plates. After they had cleared the table, Bryn said goodnight and headed out to the open barn in the courtyard, where he bedded down in the straw between his dappled mare, Betsy, and a snoring Wesley.

"Bryn likes to sleep where he can see the stars," said Orin as he closed the castle doors.

"Won't his wife wonder where he is?" asked Alfie.

The druid's smile faded a little. "Bryn's wife died over ten years ago, but he keeps her alive by talking about her. In his heart she is always with him."

A pang of sadness plucked at Alfie's heart as he remembered Bryn had mentioned his wife the very first time they had met. Alfie's mum had died several years ago, and while he thought of her nearly every day, he still found it hard to talk about her too much.

"Now, I must bid you goodnight," said Orin. "I have some reading to do before bed."

"I think an early night for everyone is in order," said Ashford, as the druid retired to his study.

"OK, OK, we're going," said Alfie as the butler shooed them all upstairs.

Alfie had chosen the room that would become his own bedroom in the future – it contained two smaller canopied beds rather than his huge four-poster – and Robin was going to share with him rather than using his own room. Amy and Madeleine were sharing too.

"Are you taking your usual bedroom, Ash?" asked Amy.

"Certainly not!" grinned Ashford, as he chose a room further down the corridor. "I can't be seen to be staying below stairs while I'm on holiday. Anyone might think I was a butler!"

4

Alfie's Sword

Alfie was rudely awoken by a cockerel crowing down in the courtyard. It seemed to start up again each time he tried to go back to sleep. He got out of bed and pressed the knot in the woodwork that opened the secret entrance to his huge bathroom. Nothing happened.

"Guess you don't have an en-suite bathroom in this century," said Robin, rubbing his eyes blearily. Alfie sighed and plodded along the corridor to investigate the main bathroom, worried that he hadn't seen one on their tour. Fortunately it was still there, but quite different to the one at home. The huge bath with its dials and wooden shower canopy was gone. In its place was a large hand pump connected to what looked like a copper showerhead hanging from the ceiling.

He went back to get Robin and they took it in turns to stand under the shower in their swimming trunks while the other worked the water pump. Alfie rubbed himself down quickly with a bar of herbal soap under the icy water, the suds draining away down little channels in the floor.

"It might be cold, but this is pretty amazing for medieval times," panted Robin as he pumped the water. "I thought we'd be washing in a barrel outside!"

Gasping and shivering as he darted out from under the shower, Alfie began to rub his arms briskly with a fluffy towel he had brought from home. He'd happily have bathed outside with the sheep if there was a chance of warm water.

Orin had said that they could dress in their usual clothes within the confines of the castle, at least until Bryn brought them some medieval clothes. The second Alfie unzipped his case to get his jeans, a pair of his boxer shorts shot up into the air and began to fly erratically around the room. He watched open-mouthed as the flying underwear bumped into walls and bedposts.

"What is it? Magic?" asked Robin, ducking as the pants swooped over the top of his head.

"Oh, no!" said Alfie as the pants began to chirp. "I don't believe it!" He grabbed them as they flew past and wrestled them down on to the floor as something struggled to free itself from the underwear. Finally, a little silver bird untangled itself from the elastic and flew up to perch on a bedpost. It ruffled its feathers, and began to chirp happily down at Alfie and Robin.

"Sparky! What are *you* doing here?" cried Alfie, unable to believe that it had the intelligence to stow away in his luggage.

The bird looked at Alfie with its head cocked to one side.

"Don't try that cute thing with me! If Artan couldn't come, there's no way you should be here either." He shook his finger angrily at the little bird. Taking Alfie's pointing finger for a perch, Sparky fluttered down to land on it and chirped a little melody, as though thoroughly proud of itself.

Working together, Alfie and Robin managed to coax the bird into their wardrobe. Alfie tied the door firmly shut to stop it flying around the castle and appearing to Orin before it had been presented to him by the great da Vinci.

"Dad's going to be looking all over for that little idiot!" he sighed. "Come on, let's get breakfast."

Madeleine and Amy were already down in the kitchens with Orin and Bryn, tucking into porridge laced with honey and berries. Alfie ladled out a large bowl for himself and Robin. Ashford didn't appear until they had scraped their bowls clean.

"I'd almost forgotten what a lie-in felt like," he grinned. "I think I'll spend this afternoon enjoying the sun in the courtyard while you begin your lessons."

"Well, I guess you'll need to warm up after that icy shower," said Alfie, noticing his wet hair.

"Cold? It was lovely and warm. Once the fire in the Great Hall is lit the water gets good and hot."

He laughed at Alfie and Robin's faces. "You forget, I've been here before. Eighty years from now, but the plumbing is the same. I must show you how to charge the pump so that showering isn't a two-person job."

"You could have told us yesterday!" Alfie called after him as Ashford grabbed a bowl of porridge and practically skipped outside to eat it, whistling as he went.

"I think I hate Holiday Ashford," muttered Robin.

Bryn left straight after breakfast. Orin led them up to the library and handed Amy and the twins a large hand-made book full of drawings of flowers and herbs.

"This contains all of my studies so far on magical and medicinal plants. Take it and see how many plants you can identify down in my herb garden. I will be particularly impressed if you can memorize some of the uses of the ones you find."

Robin hugged the book to his chest and hurried ahead of the other two as if it was a competition he was desperate to win.

"Shouldn't I go with them and study herbs?" asked Alfie as their voices died away in the corridor. He had already looked through some of Orin's books to try and get a head start on his studies, but still found it very difficult to remember the different uses of any of the herbs and flowers. He was very worried that Orin would think he was stupid.

"Later," said Orin. "First, I was hoping we could spend a little time talking about the magic that you guard."

Alfie followed Orin into his study and sat on the stool by the fire, wondering what the druid had to say. Orin settled into the armchair and twisted one of the plaits in his beard around his finger.

"Alfie. In a few months you turn thirteen. This is the age when any magical abilities a person might have become stronger. I hid the ancient creation magic inside you when you were barely an hour old. It was to hibernate inside you until you reached the age of thirteen ... or so I thought."

"So why have I been able to feel it?" asked Alfie. "It's like it wants me to use it whenever I'm in trouble." He tried not to think about the insistent whispering voices that rose in his head whenever the magic asked to be used.

"I didn't foresee this," said Orin. "It is why the castle was passed to you over a year before it was supposed to, and why your training is beginning early. The Fates are tricky creatures. When they advised me to pass the magic on to you to hide it from those who sought it, they kept much from me. For one, they did not tell me that you had abilities of your own."

"What do you mean, abilities of my own?" Alfie knew he was a pretty good artist, but he had a feeling this wasn't the ability the druid was talking about.

"In my very first letter I told you that the magic would become more active inside you when you reach the age of thirteen. Well, not only did it awaken, but you used it."

Alfie thought back to the moment when the magic had burst out of his chest and into the gigantic dragon that had threatened him and his family. It had stripped away the creature's change magic and left it trapped in the two human forms it had occupied for many years: Alfie's head teachers, Murkle and Snitch.

"I feared to tell you this, but that much power pouring through one so young. . ." He paused and shook his head. "Alfie, it should have torn you apart."

"WHAT?" Alfie nearly fell off his stool. "You're serious? Did you know that when you used me as a hiding place?"

"I'm so sorry. Of course I didn't know. You should never have been able to use it. An ordinary child should not have been able to notice it locked away inside. Especially with the talisman to dampen down any trace of its existence."

"That worked well then, didn't it?" said Alfie. "It's already nearly killed me about three times."

Orin rubbed his temple and sighed. "Alfie, you are far from ordinary. The magic woke because its strength is amplified within you. It recognizes that you could use it in ways that others who dream only of its power could never comprehend."

"I don't understand this," said Alfie. "You told me that the magic shouldn't be used. What does this all mean?"

"The Fates tricked me. I would never have hidden the magic inside you if I had known."

"Known *what*?" Alfie felt hot as he tried to keep his hands from clenching into fists. Orin was scaring him. What was he trying to say?

"The Fates spoke to me again seven days ago. You are not just a hiding place for the magic. It is your sword."

"My sword? You mean I'm supposed to use it as a weapon?" His heart seemed to stop for a second. "Against what exactly?"

"I ... I don't know, they would not say. All I know is that I must to teach you to use it."

Alfie stared at Orin, open-mouthed. "After everything you said about keeping it contained, and that using it could have blown me apart – now you want me to learn how to use it, because of something you can't even tell me about? You're joking, right?"

Orin sat with his head in his hands for a while.

"It was destiny that brought the magic to you,

Alfie. The Fates have a plan for you. Whatever either of us do will not change that. All I can do is teach you how to use the magic for when the time comes. Will you let me teach you?"

Alfie's head was reeling as he stared at Orin. He had thought this was going to be a fun trip with his cousins. Now Orin was telling him he had to learn to use the magic inside him as a weapon, and couldn't even tell him against what, or when!

"Sorry," he muttered, getting up so quickly the stool toppled over. "Need to think." He rushed through the door into the library, blindly slamming it behind him. Racing over to the window he threw it wide and took in big lungfuls of cool air, concentrating very hard on not being sick. If he could have ripped the magic out of his chest and hurled it down into Lake Archelon he would have done so. He leaned his head against the window frame, grateful that Orin hadn't tried to follow him.

Amy and the twins were down in the courtyard below. He watched them as he tried to calm his thumping heart. Robin had taken control of Orin's book and seemed to be arguing with Madeleine, who was waving a bunch of herbs under his nose and stabbing her finger on to the page as though making a point. Amy had given up on the exercise and was lying on the ground swishing her arms and legs up and down to create an angel shape in the straw strewn across the cobbles. Ashford was lying on the grass by the pond munching an apple as he read a book. He seemed set on making the most of his two weeks of freedom without Caspian's raven sentinels watching from the castle walls and reporting back to the solicitor.

Alfie chewed his thumbnail as he watched them all down in the courtyard. They had always been there for each other. When the dragon Murkle and Snitch had tried to incinerate him in the village square, Madeleine and Robin had tried to distract it. Ashford had been shot with an arrow when trying to keep Alfie's talisman a secret. Amy had given herself up to a room full of armed elves in order to try and save Robin. There were so many ways they had all stood up for and saved each other that Alfie could barely count them all.

He sat up and took a deep breath. Well, if something *was* coming, something that could hurt everyone he cared about, he would be ready to stop it.

Orin was standing by the window when Alfie

slipped back into the study. He joined the druid at the window and looked out across Hexbridge. The druid didn't say anything, but Alfie knew what he was feeling. He looked suddenly older, sorrow and guilt tracing their lines across his usually happy face.

Alfie put his hand on the druid's arm. "You couldn't have known what would and could happen. But you can help me to prepare. Please, teach me."

5

The Stone and the Hare

Orin placed a candle on the table by the window and motioned for Alfie to sit down opposite him.

"Do you want me to meditate again?" asked Alfie.

"No, but it will help with this task if you try to clear your mind as you do during that exercise."

Alfie nodded and allowed himself to slip into the relaxed state of mind he had spent weeks practising. He seemed more aware of everything in that state: the slight breeze from the window, the scent of the burning wax and the gentle heat of the flame.

"When your magic stripped away the dragon's

change magic, it did so through the talisman you wear to control it. We're going to try something much smaller, so you won't need to use the talisman. Hold your left hand out to the candle, not too close, just enough to feel its heat. We usually take with the left hand, and give with the right."

The warmth of the candle tickled Alfie's fingers as he held them a little way above the dancing flame.

"You have used the magic before. Can you feel where it lies inside you?"

In his relaxed state, Alfie paid attention to the centre of his chest. He didn't think about the magic often as it gave him nightmares, but he could feel it there, coiled up small like a hibernating snake. It seemed to twitch as he focussed his attention on it.

"At the moment you are just feeling the warmth of the candle against your skin. Imagine yourself drawing the heat energy from it. Feel it flow up your arm; guide it towards the magic."

The candle began to flicker as Alfie focussed. A gentle warmth began to penetrate his hand. He could feel the magic uncoil slightly as the heat ran up his arm towards it. The candle flame died lower and lower, finally winking out.

"What happened?" he asked as a thin stream of

smoke floated up from the extinguished candle. But he already knew. He had fed his magic on the energy from the flame. He could feel its disappointment at such a small meal.

"You fed the magic once before, when you stripped the change magic from the dragon. Caspian informed me that Ashford drew that energy from you to rebuild the fallen tower, so am I right in thinking you have never used it to create anything yourself?"

Alfie shook his head. He hadn't dared.

"Today I will teach you how. We'll start with something small." He took a smooth pebble with a hole in it from the windowsill and placed it before Alfie. "Duplicate it."

"You want me to create a copy of that?" said Alfie, looking from the stone to the druid. "How?"

"Communicate with the magic inside you," said Orin. "Tell it what you want. Guide it."

Alfie pushed his hair out of his eyes as he tried to figure out exactly what the druid wanted him to do. Finally he held both hands out in front of him, palms facing each other and the fingertips of each hand almost touching. Staring hard at the little stone, he reached out to the magic inside him. He felt a strange spark from it, almost as though the magic was excited at being given something to do.

A tingle ran down Alfie's arms and into his fingertips. Unsure of what else to do, he focussed on the empty space between them. He felt a pins-and-needles sensation in his fingertips and almost jumped up in surprise when tiny tendrils of light emerged from them.

"Good. Keep focussed," said Orin.

Alfie's heart beat faster as something began to happen to the air between his fingers. It was almost as if there were an invisible version of the stone floating there and the tendrils were flowing around it, following its shape. Slowly it gained in substance, turning over and over as colour flowed through it, mimicking the stone on the table down to the last little chip.

The stone dropped to the table with a clatter that made Alfie jump. He picked it up and turned it over. It was warm to the touch and absolutely perfect down to the weight and texture.

"Astonishing!" whispered Orin, eyes wide. "I wanted to see what you would do, rather than guide you. You used it so naturally – it took me weeks to be able to do just that." He pulled at his beard. "It could be down to the fact the magic has been with you all of your life, but I believe that the Fates are right. It was passed to you because you are the one person that can wield and control it."

Alfie barely heard Orin's words as he rubbed his thumb over the stone. His eyes flicked up to meet Orin's. "What else can I do?" he asked.

Orin lit the candle many times over the next couple of hours. By lunchtime the table was covered with stones, marbles, thimbles, keys – Alfie didn't want to stop. The magic felt less snake-like to him now; it was almost like a puppy wagging its tail with excitement at the prospect of being let off the leash.

"I think it's time we stopped for lunch," said the druid as a small and intricate shell dropped from Alfie's hands on to the almost overflowing table.

Alfie glanced at the flames flickering in the fireplace, wondering what he could create with so much more energy. Orin placed his hand on his arm.

"That's enough for now," he said quietly.

Alfie blinked and shook his head, realizing that everything but the flame and objects he was creating had almost faded out of existence while he had been working.

"Addictive, isn't it?" said the druid. "Remember,

you must be the one in control. You should never let the magic use *you*."

For lunch, Ashford had prepared a picnic – a delicious salad with herbs and fruit from the garden, and cheese and nuts from the storeroom. He had even found time to bake a loaf of bread and a fruit cake.

"I might be on holiday, but I don't want to get too out of practice," he grinned.

They ate in the shade of the oak tree in the courtyard. Robin was keen to show off what he had learnt and insisted that Orin test them on the names of the herbs they had been studying. Orin showed them pictures of the herbs, covering the names with his hand. One by one Robin reeled off the answers:

"Angelica. Sage. Lovage. Horehound. Mandrake."

"Well done, Robin!" said the druid, closing the book.

Alfie noticed Madeleine roll her eyes as her brother seemed to swell with pride.

"Now, a different test. It is easy enough to memorize a picture, but can you find the plants for yourself among many others? I would like you to pick a St John's Wort flower for me."

Robin dashed off across the courtyard, scouring the herb garden and flowerbeds. Madeleine sat and watched him. Amy, not having bothered studying, used the opportunity to pinch half a boiled egg from Robin's plate.

After wandering to and fro for ages, Robin finally returned with a small yellow flower. Madeleine took one look at it and shook her head.

"That's a buttercup. They both have five petals, but they're longer on St John's Wort and it has longer stamens. There's a plant, over there by the wall, next to the rhubarb."

Robin stared at Madeleine as though she had just started speaking an alien language.

"Very good, Madeleine," said Orin. "And can either of you tell me some of its uses?"

Robin stared blankly, so Madeleine piped up. "It's good for when you're feeling sad, and for treating inflammation. But I find arnica, that little yellow flower there that looks like a dandelion, and witch hazel better for swelling and cuts and bruises."

At this point Alfie and Amy were just as surprised as Robin.

"But you hardly looked at the book!" cried Robin.

Madeleine shrugged. "Didn't need to. Gran has been telling us this stuff for years, but you don't pay attention because it doesn't come from a book. Besides, that balm that Orin made to cure Ashford's wound was amazing. I wanted to try and find out what was in it, so I've been experimenting." She pulled a little pot of yellowish green paste from her pocket. "It's nowhere near as good as yours," she told Orin sheepishly. "But it's great for spots!"

Robin stared at her with newfound admiration and a touch of jealousy as Orin unscrewed the lid and sniffed the paste.

"There's a strong scent there that I don't recognize."

"That's tea tree. It's from another country right around the other side of the world. It hasn't been discovered yet, well, except by all the Aboriginal people already living on it, but for some reason history doesn't count them!" she added.

"And tell me, Madeleine. If you were to brew a soothing tisane for someone who had suffered a great fright, what would you put in it?"

"You mean like a tea?" She scratched her chin. "Well, I guess I'd use dried chamomile, St John's Wort, some lemon balm, maybe a bit of honey to make it taste nice too. If they were feeling sick I'd add peppermint, and if they were having trouble sleeping I'd use valerian, ooh, and hops."

Orin clapped his hands. "Well, who would have thought we have a natural healer in our midst!" He laughed delightedly as Alfie clapped Madeleine on the back.

Robin crossed his arms and Alfie heard him mutter just under his breath, "Not me!"

Amy and the twins were given the rest of the afternoon off, which was just as well – Robin's excitement for learning about herbs and medicinal plants had gone flat in the light of Madeleine's surprising knowledge in the area. He had gone back to reading more of Orin's writings on enchantments and potion mixing while Madeleine had set up some targets in the courtyard and was teaching Amy archery. Ashford had knocked some wood together to make himself an easel and set it up on the battlements to paint the village below.

"So what are we going to do?" Alfie asked Orin. "Are we going back to practising with the magic?" He thought hungrily of the roaring fire in the druid's study.

"We are," said Orin. "But in a different way. I want to show you why it is so dangerous, and why you must keep control of it – no matter how great the temptation to do bigger things grows."

Leaving the twins applauding Amy's efforts with a longbow, Alfie followed the druid to a large stone sundial in a sheltered corner of the courtyard. He had often wondered why a sundial had been placed in the corner out of the sun, but had assumed that it had once stood in the centre of the courtyard.

"After you," said Orin.

Alfie looked blankly at the sundial on its thick stone pillar, then back up at the druid. "You want me to tell the time?"

Orin laughed. "So you haven't discovered everything about our castle yet? Well then, this is going to be fun. I created this castle in 1389; grasp the brass arm in the centre of the dial and turn it to the numbers that make up that year."

Alfie did as the druid asked, very thankful that they had just covered Roman numerals in history class. There was a little click as the arm stopped on each of the numbers, I, III, VIII. . . When he twisted it to the final number, IX, there was a clunk. The dial rotated back to its starting point and the whole plinth slid aside with a grinding noise. Beneath it was a gaping hole.

The druid sat down, dangling his legs into the hole. "Meet you at the bottom!"

With that, he was gone.

Amy and the twins were hard at practice, not even looking in his direction. Alfie peered down into the darkness, but Orin was long gone. He sat down, took a deep breath and let himself drop into the hole. He was very glad he had taken a breath as he suddenly found himself whizzing down a chute so fast that he couldn't even yell. Fear very quickly gave way to exhilaration as he shot through the darkness flat on his back. Finally he saw light, and a second later he hurtled out of a hole and into a springy bed of heather down by Lake Archelon.

"That..." he shouted as he bounced himself out of the heather, which sprang back to hide the chute from prying eyes, "was brilliant! Can we do it again?"

But the druid was already untying a small wooden boat moored to a small jetty. He threw Alfie a long cloak.

"Better wear this over your clothes now that we're outside."

Alfie tied the cloak around his neck and pretended to fly towards the boat like a superhero, much to Orin's bemusement. Together they rowed out to one of the small tree-ringed islands in the centre of the lake. Alfie had sailed out to them a couple of times with Amy and the twins for picnics. The trees and bushes made the islands feel shut off from the rest of the world, except for the odd duck or swan that waddled over to demand a share of the food. Orin tied up the boat and led the way to a tiny clearing in the centre, obscured from view of the land. They sat down among the plants.

"Why are we here?" asked Alfie, pushing aside a large fern so that he could see the druid.

"You have seen how your magic can draw upon energy, such as heat," said Orin. "Now you must see what else it can feed on. That fern you are touching, what can you feel from it?"

Alfie squeezed the fronds with his fingers. "It feels a bit rough."

"No. Clear your mind as we have practised and feel deeper, with your mind as well as your fingers."

Alfie did as the druid asked. He concentrated on the fern, letting all else slip away. It didn't take long before he felt it – the life force of the plant. Soon it was vibrating through his fingers; he could almost feel the cells inside it working industriously.

"Now," said Orin, "draw out that energy, just as you did with the flame."

Alfie could feel the magic, awake and alert inside him. He began to draw the energy from the fern up his arm towards his chest. It felt different to the flame, so much more powerful, a pulsating vibrant energy. He wondered what he could create with it, and was so wrapped up in the glorious sensation of power running up his arm that he did not notice what was happening to the plant. Only when the last little shiver of energy had been drawn from it did he notice that the fern was grey, drained of colour and life. As he jerked his hand away, the entire plant crumbled, like dust.

"How do you feel?" asked Orin.

Alfie stared at the last remnants of the fern drifting away on the breeze. "I didn't mean to kill it," he said. The magic inside him seemed to be humming with excitement, waiting to be used. "It's different, isn't it? The energy from plants is more powerful than the heat I took from the flame."

Orin nodded. "Why do you think that is?"

Alfie remembered the sensation as he had touched the fern, the life pulsing through its leaves.

"It's life, isn't it? Heat is energy, but it's not alive. Life energy is stronger. The magic seemed to want it more."

Orin nodded.

"The fern – can I recreate it?" asked Alfie, running the dust through his fingers.

"Give it a try."

Alfie licked his lips and held his right hand out over the spot where the fern had stood. The magic was easier to use every time. He didn't even need to concentrate on the exact appearance of what he was creating; it was as though the magic knew exactly what it should look like and filled in all the details. The little strands of magical energy danced from his fingers, building a fine network of veins, and then the leaves of the plant. The magic inside Alfie practically sang as he worked – it made him feel powerful. Special. He had a skill that no one else held, and he could use it for so much!

As the leaves lost their transparency and turned a rich green, Alfie stopped the magic flowing and felt it retreat back into his chest.

"There," he said, sitting back and admiring the plant. "Good as new!"

"Is it?" asked Orin.

Alfie looked at the fern. It seemed perfect to him, no different to the others in the clearing.

"Touch it," said Orin.

Alfie stroked one of the leaves. Something felt

odd. "The texture . . . it isn't quite right," he said at last.

Orin seemed to want something else from him, but Alfie wasn't sure what. He looked at the other ferns. They all *looked* the same as his. Holding on to one of the fronds, he reached out and touched another plant. Instantly he recoiled from both ferns. He knew what was wrong.

"It's dead! It looks like a real plant, but there's no life in it." He flexed his fingers. "I've still got some of the energy from it; I can make it so that it's alive again, can't I?"

"No, Alfie. You can't. Organic matter is impossible to truly replicate. I'm amazed you created a copy so close. But however realistic you make something, the magic cannot create life; it can only feed on it."

Alfie stared at the fern. It looked ugly to him now, an impostor sitting among the live plants.

"Now, I have one more lesson for you," said Orin. He began to whistle softly, the same few notes, over and over. Eventually there was a rustling sound, and a pair of large yellow eyes appeared at the far side of the clearing. Orin reached into the pouch on his belt and pulled out a handful of leafy herbs. He held them out and whistled again. A large hare bounded out of the bushes and over to the druid, where it stopped and nibbled gently at the herbs in his hand.

"He's so tame!" gasped Alfie.

"She's not, but she knows her friends," smiled the druid. He handed Alfie some of the herbs. The hare stood up on her back legs, nose twitching as Alfie tried to coax her over to him. Finally she hopped towards him and began to eat from his hands. Alfie grinned up at Orin.

"Can I stroke her?"

"Perhaps she will let you."

Alfie reached out his hand ever so slowly, half afraid that the hare would bolt for the trees, but it continued munching on the leaves, pulling them one by one from his hand. Finally, his fingertips brushed its fur. It was coarse, not soft and fluffy like the rabbits he had stroked in pet shops, but it was more beautiful somehow.

The druid's eyes were fixed on Alfie's, as though searching for something.

Alfie could feel the hare breathing as he gently ran his fingers down her side, but more than that, he could feel the life blazing through it – it was an exhilarating sensation. A sudden pang in his chest made him gasp as whispers he had heard before began to build in his head. The magic was hungry; it could feel the life force of the hare and it wanted it. He felt it reaching out through him, creeping down towards his fingers as the hare munched away, oblivious to the danger. Orin was watching him carefully. Did the druid know what was happening inside of him? Is that why he had called the hare?

The whispers in Alfie's head grew more insistent, hinting that he could have anything he wanted – all he had to do was let the magic feed. His arm began to shake as he held back, fighting against the hunger, dragging the magic back from its prey.

"No!" he shouted at last, snatching his hand back as though it had been burnt. Startled, the hare bounded away into the undergrowth. Alfie flopped back on to the grass, panting as he held his hand tight to his chest.

"You see now?" said the druid softly. "Why the magic is so dangerous?"

"Life," panted Alfie. "Real living things – that's where it gets the most power. You knew, didn't you? After all that practice today, you knew it would want the hare?"

"Yes," said Orin. "But I also knew that you would not let it take it. It thinks that you want power and material things. It does not understand that you are happy, you do not need the things it whispers of. Most others would be easily corrupted by it."

"But I nearly. . ."

"But you *didn't*!" said Orin. "You didn't."

Alfie was glad that the druid left him to his own thoughts as they rowed back to the shore and climbed the hill to the castle in silence. Visions of the hare crumbling away to dust beneath his hand swam through his mind. He made himself a promise that he would never use the magic on a living thing again.

6

The Prophecy and the Dream

Bryn was back at the castle that evening, bringing a delicious stew with dumplings. He had everyone in stitches as they ate with a story about the night Wesley the goat had eaten a hole in the seat of his trousers as he slept in the stable. Alfie smiled along, but he was still very bothered by the experience with the hare. He barely tasted the stew he was spooning into his mouth as he heard Robin questioning Orin on the pronunciation of some of the runic words in the books he had borrowed. Alfie couldn't even get through a couple of lines of the text in those books, but Robin was flying through them, and Madeleine already seemed to be an expert in herbology and healing potions. Maybe Orin should have picked one of them to be his apprentice.

Alfie was glad when everyone decided to go to bed straight after dinner.

"You're quiet tonight," said Robin as they climbed into their beds. "Orin's so clever, isn't he? I'm learning so much from his books. What did he teach you today – was it something to do with your magic?"

"Just some stuff," mumbled Alfie. A little twinge of jealousy ran through him as he watched Robin light an oil lamp and settle back into his pillows with another of Orin's books. How could he lie there reading those as easily as if they were comics?

"I'm going to find something to read," he said sharply, jumping out of bed and hurrying from the room. He didn't really want a book – he just had to get away from Robin and his big stupid brain. The flagstones under his feet seemed to cool his temper as he headed to the library, angry at himself for feeling envious of his cousin.

The library and Orin's study were dark. Alfie leafed through a few pages of a book on the druid's desk. It was full of Orin's calligraphic writing, but the languages switched between Latin, French and runes. Even the bits in English were hard enough for Alfie to understand. He sighed. He was learning to handle the magic, but wasn't sure he'd ever come close to learning everything else Orin wanted to teach him. Would the druid be angry if Alfie couldn't be the apprentice he had hoped for? Would he leave the castle to someone else instead?

Alfie wandered back into the library, clapping his hands so that the torches on the walls burst into flame. He flopped into one of the chairs by the fireplace and glared up at the Fates. The three wooden women stared impassively over the spinning wheel on which they span the fate of mortals. Clotho, the youngest, spinning the thread of life; her sister Lachesis, measuring it to decide how long a person will live; and the old woman, Atropos, holding her scissors over the thread, ready to cut a life short.

"Well?" he asked them. "You seem to have all these plans for me. Fancy actually telling me something about them? Or are you just going to sit there gathering dust?"

It was nearly a year since the one and only time Alfie had heard the Fates speak. He didn't expect a reply, so when the spinning wheel began to turn with a creak and a crack, all of his bravado disappeared. He gulped and clutched the arms of the chair as the voices of the Fates bypassed his ears to arrive directly in his head.

> He stops, he stares. We know he cares, for
> > family and friends,
> But for their souls a shadow comes,
> > through the night it wends.
> Death is roaming through these lands, its
> > presence growing stronger,
> As we sing it searches wide, its master
> > waits no longer.

> Does he wield the magic well, or is he in its
> > thrall?
> Will he choose to keep it safe, or will he
> > lose it all?
> Kin will stand close by his side, their help
> > he must enlist,
> Will he see what he should know? – Four
> > fingers make a fist.

> Though some foes have been vanquished,
> > there will be many still,
> The magic must become his sword,
> > tempered by his will.

Good will take up arms again, an age-old
war to fight,
But inner battles must be fought when
magic lends its might."

The third verse Alfie recognized. It had changed
a little, but he had heard parts of it before – the
first time the Fates spoke to him. Their prophecy
had come true. After Murkle and Snitch had come
the elves, and that wasn't the end. He didn't dare to
think about what else could follow. He had already
experienced inner battles against the magic as it
had begged to be used. He knew he would always
be fighting those voices if he was to learn to use the
magic. The earlier verses worried him even more: a
shadow coming through the night, death roaming
the land, doubt cast on his ability to wield the magic.
He shivered and grabbed a torch from the wall – he
didn't feel like walking back to bed in the darkness.

Robin was already asleep, the book lying over
his face. Alfie gently removed it and laid it on the
nightstand before climbing into his own bed. He
left the candles and torch lit to try to drive away
the chill of the Fates' words as he fell into a restless
sleep.

*

The wraith had wandered far, but was no closer to fulfilling the purpose for which it had been torn from its grave. It had tried to return to the great sleep, sinking into the soil of an ancient burial ground within the blackland, but its master's command would not let it rest; it must keep searching.

Rising from the comforting earth and up through the heather, the wraith hovered in the centre of a stone circle. It began to fade until it was almost lost in the inky night as it sent its wisps reaching out, sniffing ... searching ... feeling for *It* – for the magic. This time was different. Something in the land had changed. The vibration was faint, almost as if hidden or protected by something, but the wraith could sense it – the magic was back. It had been used recently, and though there was still a protection around it, traces lingered where it had last been used. The destination was clear at last.

The wraith shuddered with the effort of recalling its brothers and sisters. It needed more strength, more life – it must borrow from the living again. It would do this on the way. Turning towards Hexbridge, it began its journey.

*

Alfie was wrenched from sleep by a chilling noise

from the next bedroom. Someone was screaming. Robin was already up and running for the door, Alfie raced after him into the girls' room.

Amy was sitting on her bed, hugging her knees. Her face was pale and her hair was plastered to her forehead with sweat.

Madeleine was filling a glass of water from the jug on the dresser, and spilt half of it in her mad dash back to Amy.

Amy took the water and gulped it down gratefully as Madeleine stroked her hair.

"What's going on?" asked Alfie, looking swiftly around the room. He had never seen Amy look so shaken before. "Has someone been in here? Are you ill?"

"She had a nightmare," said Madeleine.

Amy finished the water and took a deep shuddering breath. "It wasn't a nightmare. I … I don't know what it was. I wasn't myself – I was this thing made out of shadows and voices, all of them cold and frightened. I was out on the moors searching for something."

"For what?" Alfie asked.

Amy shook her head. "I'm not sure. I'd been looking for days and then finally I knew where it was. Here, in Hexbridge." She shivered. "When I woke up I really felt as though it was still coming here. But that wasn't the worst part. I ... it was cold and weak. It seemed to be drawn to life and warmth. It came to a tiny village and drifted from house to house, drawing black crosses on to the doors with its finger. Each time, I could feel more warmth rush into it, as though it became a little bit more alive with each cross. When I passed the window of one of the houses, I could see why..."

She hugged her legs tighter as Madeleine stroked her back.

"The villagers – they were frozen, eyes open. Not quite dead, but it was like the life had just been sucked out of them."

Alfie rubbed his arm as it came up in goose-pimples when he remembered the words of the Fates:

> Death is roaming through these lands,
>   its presence growing stronger,
> As we sing it searches wide, its master
>   waits no longer.

"Don't worry," said Robin. "I'm sure it was just a dream. Maybe it was a side effect of that potion Orin gave us?"

"I wish I could believe that," said Amy. "But it

felt real. Too real."

Alfie wasn't used to seeing Amy frightened. The dream had really affected her. "Come on," he said. "Let's go tell Orin about it."

The druid was out in the courtyard garden, milking the cow while Wesley chewed one of the corners of his tunic. Bryn was chopping wood nearby, hefting large logs around as though they were matchsticks. The woodsman seemed amused by the girls' pyjamas and the boys' dressing gowns.

"And here was I thinking that those long pointed shoes and codpieces the nobles wear were as strange as fashion can get!" He chuckled to himself and went back to chopping wood.

Orin stopped milking and listened intently to Amy's story. The hairs on the back of Alfie's neck prickled as he saw how seriously the druid seemed to be taking the dream.

"This town. . ." he said as she finished. "Do you know its name?"

Amy shook her head. "It was just about five wooden houses around a crossroads. There was a river nearby, if that helps?"

"That could be one of many towns," said Orin, pulling at his beard. "Can you tell me anything else?"

Amy bit her lip as she thought. "There was a bigger town just before it. It had a monastery, a dairy and farm animals – lots of farm animals. I could feel them nearby, but it wasn't interested in them. Just the people."

Bryn had stopped chopping wood. "Sounds like Miggleswick, 'bout thirteen miles south of here."

"I thought so too," said Orin.

"You're saying Amy dreamt about a real town?" said Robin. "How is that possible? She doesn't know the towns around Hexbridge, especially not in medieval times!"

"My dream, it wasn't ... real, was it?" asked Amy.

"Perhaps not," said Orin. "But the most vivid of dreams should never be ignored."

"The dream isn't all," said Alfie. "The Fates spoke to me again last night." Amy and the twins stared as he told the druid what they had said about death roaming the land. Orin's brow furrowed as he listened. He turned to the woodsman. "Bryn..."

"Right ahead of you, Orin. I'll take Betsy and check the hamlets around Miggleswick. I'll be back by dusk."

"Thank you," said Orin as Bryn hurried away to

saddle up his horse.

"Now then," said the druid, looking down at their four worried faces. "Bryn will look into it. In the meantime, there's no point worrying and wondering when there's work to be done."

The druid handed out chores. Robin finished milking the cows while Amy and Alfie collected eggs and fed the chickens, and Madeleine raked out the stable. Alfie was very hungry for breakfast by the time they had finished. They all trooped into the kitchen in their dirty pyjamas. Ashford had stepped out of holiday mode to cook up scrambled eggs served on toasted rye bread. He had even brewed up a very strong pot of tea from a bag of black tea leaves that he had smuggled into the past with them.

"I know it won't be available for two hundred years yet," he said as he stirred a large spoon of honey into Amy's cup, "but if that doesn't make you feel better, nothing will!"

"Thanks, Ash," said Amy. She took a sip and flashed him a smile.

Alfie thought she looked a lot more like her usual self after helping Orin out with the chores. The druid always seemed to know how to make things better.

"Right then," said Orin, as they finished their eggs and washed the plates in the stone sink. "Time to get dressed so that we can get back to lessons. Hold on!" he shouted after them as they all dashed for the stairs. "You'll need your new clothes."

They followed the druid into the Great Hall. On the table were bundles containing tunics, leggings, cloaks and jerkins. Madeleine's bundle was a little different.

"Oh, no. No way," she cried, holding up a long woollen dress and a wimple. "How come I get these and Amy gets trousers?"

Alfie knew it was more than his life was worth to let out the laugh that was building inside him. Orin had gone a little pink under his beard.

"Bryn fetched them from a seamstress in the village this morning. He, er, well ... that is to say he thought with Amy's short hair and build she would be best suited to boy's clothes."

"Fine by me," said Amy, holding her trousers against her waist for size. Her unease at her dream seemed to have disappeared next to Madeleine's horrified expression as she unwrapped a bodice.

"It's just for travelling outside the castle," said Orin quickly. "You may wear your own garments within its walls."

"It's a good job we took that potion," growled Madeleine. "Because I'm thinking about my wardrobe back at home pretty hard right now!"

Half an hour later, they were all showered and dressed and seated in Orin's study ready to continue their lessons. Everyone except Madeleine had been keen to try their new clothes. Alfie liked his linen shirt and waistcoat, but the coarse trousers had him wanting to scratch his legs constantly. However uncomfortable he felt in the trousers, he had to admit that it didn't come close to Madeleine's discomfort. Amy had talked her into wearing the long gown with the lace-up bodice and skirt over the top. She was squirming around and pulling at it as if someone had emptied a bucket of spiders over her. In fact, Alfie thought she'd probably be much happier wearing a bucket of spiders.

"Sorry, Madds," said Amy, making a frame with her fingers and squinting through one eye as though looking through a camera lens. "But this mental pic is a keeper!" She made a click noise just as Madeleine made a rude gesture at her.

Alfie was glad that Orin didn't ask him to experiment with the magic again that day. The morning was spent identifying and learning the uses for many of the herbs and strange ingredients stored in the hundreds of jars on the shelves that lined the walls of the study. After her amazing display of knowledge the day before, Alfie was hardly surprised that Madeleine was way ahead of him in this task as she examined and sniffed jar after jar, announcing their contents:

"Yarrow – good for protection, fever, stomach problems. Myrrh – calming scent, good for bad breath, toothache and lotions for cuts. Ooh, is this mandrake?"

She was holding a root that Alfie thought looked almost like a little figure with arms and legs.

"I don't know much about its uses, but Granny said people believed it screamed when it was pulled up and anyone who heard it died. She said that in the olden days people used to stay at a distance and get their dogs to pull them up."

"Oh, how nice of them!" snarled Amy.

"That's a more advanced herb that we can leave until later," said Orin as he popped it back on the shelf. "Madeleine, you suggested a recipe for a calming brew to me yesterday. Why don't you make up a draught of it for Amy while I get the others up to speed with their herbology? I'm sure she'd appreciate it after her shock this morning."

"Yeah, that would be great, Madds," said Amy.

Everyone heaved a sigh of relief as Madeleine hurried off to light the fire and gather the ingredients for the drink. Alfie gave the druid a grateful smile. He seemed to have noticed that the others had all gone quiet as Madeleine reeled off everything she knew about herbs.

Orin was a good teacher and Alfie found it a bit easier to learn the names and uses of the herbs without Madeleine leaping in first with every answer. Robin seemed desperate to show he knew just as much as his sister and got very frustrated when he kept giving the wrong answers.

The afternoon lessons were much easier for Robin, although Alfie found them to be his worst yet. Orin gave them a lesson on deciphering the runes and code words he used in his writings. Robin had already been working hard on understanding these and had many questions for Orin as they worked their way through a protection spell. Amy seemed quite back to her usual self after the brew Madeleine had made for her, but it had done nothing to spark her interest in the lessons. Alfie watched her as she idly braided a colourful shoelace into her hair and wished that he could feel so relaxed about Orin's lesson.

"Why are we learning a protection spell?" asked Madeleine. "If that thing Amy dreamed about is real, shouldn't we be learning how to fight it?"

"Attack is not the best form of defence," said the druid. "Protecting yourself and those you care about is by far the most useful skill anyone can learn and should always be the first lesson. I will teach you many forms of defence over the course of your stay here, from protecting yourselves physically, to protecting and strengthening your own minds."

"Hey, look! I think Robin did it!" said Amy.

Alfie looked at Robin, who was reciting the words from the page, his brow furrowed as he worked through the difficult words and symbols. Around him flowed fine golden strands in the shape of a protective bubble. The second Robin realized everyone was staring at him he began to stumble over the words and the golden strands evaporated.

"Brilliant!" cried Orin, clasping Robin's upper arms and shaking him proudly. "Fantastic work, we'll make druids of you all, yet!"

Maybe Robin and Madeleine, thought Alfie, but he was starting to doubt he'd ever come close to them. At least Amy wasn't making him look bad – she hadn't engaged with Orin's lessons at all. He tried his best as the afternoon dragged on, but the only one of them that managed to get anywhere with the spell was Robin. He even managed to hold the protective bubble for a few seconds as the others pelted it with scrunched-up paper and watched it bounce off.

"Hey!" cried Robin, the bubble disappearing as a pebble penetrated it and bounced off his chest. "Who's throwing stones?"

"Sorry," grinned Madeleine. "Just testing. At least you'll be safe from paper aeroplane attacks."

Ashford was coming in from the courtyard with his paints and a canvas as they went down for dinner.

"Wow, that's amazing," said Alfie as they all looked at the finished painting of the courtyard garden. "Are you going to bring it back for Emily?"

"Maybe," grinned Ashford. "Or maybe I'll leave it here to age for six hundred years and then sell it as an old masterpiece."

"I thought you were a reformed character?" said Alfie.

"There's such a thing as being too honest,"

grinned Ashford. "That's not a habit I want to fall into."

They all helped to pull together a meal consisting of fresh tomatoes and salad leaves from the garden. The salad was very tasty due to all the various herbs and edible flowers that went into it. Alfie wouldn't ever have thought about putting flowers into a salad, but the violets, rose petals and strawberries made it look as good as it tasted. Orin had made fresh bread and fried fish, and they all dived for it the second he placed the plates on the table.

"Nothing like knowledge to help you work up an appetite," laughed the druid.

Towards the end of the meal a clattering of hooves in the courtyard marked Bryn's return. Amy went out to meet him and was already deep in conversation with him by the time Alfie and the others followed.

"Orin," said Bryn, his eyes unusually serious. He nodded towards the stable and the druid and Ashford followed him over to the outbuilding where they tended to Betsy, deep in hushed conversation as the twins and Amy clustered around Alfie.

"Bryn found the place I dreamt about," said

Amy. "There were crosses on the doors of the houses and everyone inside was ill, unable to move or speak. It was just as I saw it." She shook her head, as if to shake out the mental images. "Alfie, my dream was real. What do you think it means?"

Alfie didn't even know how to start making sense of it. Amy had seen what had happened to the villagers as it actually happened. "Maybe Orin knows what it means?" But they didn't have time to ask him. As soon as he had finished talking to Bryn, he gave Madeleine a list of herbs to collect from the garden and hurried upstairs to gather together equipment from his study.

"The black crosses..." said Robin as they sat on the bench around the oak, watching Madeleine carefully cutting and packing the herbs Orin had requested. "That's what they drew on doors to mark that the people inside had the Black Death."

"You think they've got the plague?" cried Alfie, remembering the gruesome illustrations of victims of the disease in their history textbooks. He hadn't even stopped to consider the diseases that had been around in the middle ages when he had agreed to travel there.

"No, it's not the plague," said Amy. "I told you,

the thing in my dream drew the crosses; it was like it was marking where it had been."

"The thing you saw – what was it?" asked Madeleine.

Amy shook her head. "I don't know. I don't think I want to know."

7

Into the Woods

The next morning, Alfie, Amy and the twins stood at the top of the eastern tower watching Orin ride away over the hills. He had given Betsy the night to rest before setting off for the stricken village, promising to return as soon as he could. Bryn would stay with them in the castle in the meantime.

"It's a shame we couldn't bring Artan," said Madeleine as the druid finally disappeared from sight. "He could have flown Orin there in no time."

Alfie had thought they were up very early, but Bryn had already mucked out the stables and collected the hens' eggs, while Ashford had baked a fruit cake and several loaves of delicious brown bread.

"Do you think Orin will be back today?" asked Alfie between mouthfuls of poached eggs and warm buttered toast.

"He'll be back when he has done all he can for the people of Miggleswick," said Bryn. "However long that takes." He poured each of them a cup of nettle tea and sweetened it with drops of honey. "In the meantime, he has asked me to teach you what I can of the woods. The sun is already high in the sky, so we'll head out as soon as breakfast is done."

They all wolfed down the rest of their food and dashed off to get ready while Ashford packed a lunch for them. He was going to stay in the castle, in case Orin sent word back to them.

Madeleine grumbled loudly about her skirt and bodice as they trooped back downstairs. "The second I find a pair of scissors in this place, I'm cutting my hair short like Amy's," she announced.

"In that case you'd better stay here in the past," said Robin, "because Mum would kill you."

Bryn gave each of them a travelling cloak, which they enjoyed swishing around, but Madeleine continued raging over the unfairness of her clothes all the way down the hill and into the village. Alfie walked ahead with Bryn noting all of the differences in the medieval landscape – more trees, fewer houses, more of the small farm animals Alfie had seen up at the castle. There were none of the large fields of the farms in present day, instead there were lots of smaller plots growing wheat, barley and vegetables. Alfie was surprised to see that the cobbled marketplace already existed with many buildings he recognized from his own time, although all of the modern shopfronts were missing.

"There's the church, and that building there is Gertie Entwhistle's sweetshop!" Alfie marvelled at how new everything looked. The building that would eventually become the library was being rethatched; it had a slate tiled roof in Alfie's time.

"And there's the village hall," said Robin.

"We call it the Moot Hall," said Bryn. "It's where we hold all of our most important meetings, and the Beltane and Samhain feasts."

"We've got to come back for Samhain," said Amy, her eyes flashing with excitement. Alfie agreed – it would be fun to see how different the festival was six hundred years ago. After the castle and being near his cousins, the village festivals were the next best thing about living in Hexbridge.

The thatchers called down a greeting to Bryn as they passed by the future library.

"Ho there, Adam, Robert!" Bryn called back. "These are my sister's children, visiting from over Hautwysell way. My nephews, Alfred, Robert and Amery." Alfie, Robin and Amy nodded in turn as Bryn pointed to them. Alfie was very impressed at how quickly Bryn gave them medieval names. "And this is my lovely niece, Maud." Madeleine blushed beetroot red as she delivered a stiff curtsey. "Just taking them foraging."

"Mind how you go," called down Adam. "That black boar has been around again recently. Nearly gored my little Poll last week."

"I'll keep an eye out for it," called back Bryn.

"Maud? What kind of a name is Maud?" exploded Madeleine as they continued on their way.

"It was my mother's name," said Bryn. "Beautiful, isn't it?"

"Oh. Er, it's lovely," said Madeleine quickly. Alfie noticed that she said nothing further until they reached the forest.

"Are there really boar in there?" asked Alfie, peering into the dim twilight between the trees.

"There were lots of boar around in medieval times," said Robin. "I read that they were very dangerous. People were sometimes killed by them!"

Alfie suddenly felt a lot less sure about heading into the forest. He often went exploring the woods with his cousins and friends, but they seemed very different here in the 1400s. Bryn didn't seem deterred at all.

"You'll be fine with me," he grinned. "As long as they hear us coming, you won't even see any boars or wolves. Can't promise anything regarding bears though."

"BEARS? You're kidding, right?" said Amy.

"Of course he is," said Robin. "Even now, there haven't been any bears in England for a few hundred years. Isn't that right, Bryn?"

But Bryn was already striding off into the woods, whistling so loudly the air was soon filled with the noise of startled birds flapping from their nests. They hurried after him. Alfie enjoyed Bryn's bright whistle; it made the woods much less daunting. No boar would come within a mile of that cheery racket.

Alfie and the others stayed in single file behind Bryn. Although he was taking them on a well-trodden route through the woods, the ferns and thickets were trying their best to reclaim the path. Alfie's arms were getting quite scratched as brambles swung back in front of him as the giant man strode through them, calling back the names of trees and shrubs, and pointing out owl pellets and the different types of animal droppings.

"Oops. Sorry, Amy!" said Alfie as the spiky blackberry bush he had brushed past whipped back to catch her on the shins. Robin was carefully picking his way through the thicket, but Madeleine was trailing far behind, yanking her skirts out of the grip of the thorny branches and earning plenty of nettle stings on her legs in the process.

"Hey, Bryn. Wait up!" called Alfie. The woodsman turned at Alfie's shout and seemed surprised to see them all so far behind. He strode back to the group and fished several long branches out of the undergrowth, seemingly oblivious to the nettles and brambles.

"Begging your pardon," he said as he unsheathed a knife from his belt and began to strip the twigs from the branches, smoothing them into staffs. "I usually come out here alone; I forgot that you wee'uns aren't used to the wild life. There now, these should help." He handed each of them a staff and headed back along the trail. Alfie found it much easier to follow now as he used his staff to push briars and nettles out of the way.

Eventually they plunged into a clearing through which ran a gurgling stream. Bryn had already made himself comfortable on a mossy rock. He spread out his arms and beamed. "Welcome to one of my favourite thinking spots!" he announced. Alfie remembered the cosy cave in the hills where he had first encountered Bryn. He had called that one of his thinking spots too.

"It's perfect," said Madeleine, flopping down on her stomach next to the stream and cupping her hands to scoop up water. Alfie joined her, the cool water trickling down his chin and throat as he scooped it up and drank greedily.

"Delicious," he smiled.

After they had all drunk their fill and washed their scratches and stings in the cool fresh water, Madeleine pulled a roll of sticky tape from her pocket and passed them each a piece. "Stick this over your nettle stings, then pull it off," she directed. "It'll remove any nettle fibres in your skin."

Alfie did as she directed to the stings on the back of his hand and was surprised to see little white fibres on the tape as he peeled it away. The irritation eased and Madeleine passed around her pot of green paste and dock leaves to apply. It instantly cooled the burning itch.

Bryn passed out some cheese and oat biscuits. Alfie looked around the little clearing as he munched contentedly. There was a blackened area surrounded by stones where Bryn had obviously lit fires on his previous visits. The remains of a shelter sat between two trees.

"That's from the last time I spent the night here," said Bryn when he noticed Alfie looking at it.

"Do you stay out here often?" asked Robin.

"Every now and then, when I want to feel close to nature. More so these days now that. . ." his voice faltered and petered out. Alfie knew that he was thinking of his wife.

"Could you show us how to make a shelter like that?" he asked quickly.

"I certainly can," said Bryn, snapping back into the moment. "In fact, we might as well sleep out here tonight. I doubt Orin will be back until the morning at least."

Alfie felt a thrill at the thought of sleeping out in the woods. He had been camping once before, but the thought of building his own shelter filled him with excitement.

"Brilliant!" said Madeleine, leaping to her feet. "What do we need to build it?"

"Hold your horses," laughed Bryn in the face of Madeleine's eagerness. "If we're sleeping out here we should forage for our dinner tonight. Now, there are dozens of types of mushroom in this clearing alone. Do you know which ones are edible?"

Robin's eyes lit up. "I do! I've read all about them. There's wood ear, ink caps, puff balls, oyster mushrooms..."

"Very good," said Bryn. "But can you point any of those out to me?"

There were so many different types of mushroom growing from the forest floor, on rotten logs and on the trees themselves, that Alfie didn't know how anyone would be able to know which ones to eat without poisoning themselves. Robin and Madeleine immediately identified puffballs and ink caps, earning themselves high praise from the woodsman.

Alfie gazed around the clearing. The twins had an advantage in that Granny Merryweather had taught them lots about nature from an early age. Alfie and Amy had grown up in the city, and had never eaten a mushroom that hadn't been bought in a shop.

A splash of bright yellow on the bark of the tree nearest to him caught his eye. "Can you eat this one?" he asked.

"You can indeed," said Bryn, working his knife under the cluster of fat yellow fans and removing them from the tree. "They call this Chicken of the Woods, lovely in a stew."

"How about this one?" said Amy, pointing to a flat-capped mushroom that looked harmless enough to Alfie.

"That's a death cap," said Bryn. "A couple of those and you'd be dead in a week."

Amy leapt back from the mushroom as though just being near it was dangerous.

"Right then," said Bryn. "Let's have the twins on mushroom duty. Amy, you can gather blackberries and raspberries..." He paused. "You know what those look like, right?"

"Of course!" said Amy, rolling her eyes. "I'm always buying them from the supermarket for Gran to make jams."

Bryn's bushy eyebrows knitted together. "The *super*... market?" he repeated, slowly.

"It's a big shop," said Alfie. "Like, er, lots of different market stalls in one building."

"Oh, like the harvest celebration in the Moot

Hall at Samhain," said Bryn.

"Um, near enough. Now, what should I collect?" said Alfie, changing the subject rather than trying to explain food shopping in the future.

Bryn ruffled some foliage that looked like thick blades of grass. A savoury smell rose from it, warm, and slightly familiar.

"It's a bit like . . . I don't know, garlic?"

"Stinking Jenny," said Bryn. "Also known as devil's garlic – my favourite. Leave the bulbs in the earth and pick the leaves – they'll stew up lovely with the mushrooms." Alfie set to work as Bryn went to check on the mushrooms the twins were collecting. The smell of the garlic leaves was very pungent but not unpleasant. Amy foraged nearby, holding up the bottom of her tunic to create a makeshift hammock for the blackberries and raspberries she was collecting. Alfie found a big crop of wild strawberries near the garlic and added a few handfuls to Amy's berries.

By the time they had all finished, the makings of a fabulous wild feast were piled up on the sack Bryn had spread out in the centre of the clearing. Alfie's stomach was starting to rumble again, despite the cheese and biscuits.

"Well done," said Bryn after checking the berries

and mushrooms for anything poisonous. "This will make a wonderful meal. But first, we need to build our shelter for the night."

Alfie looked longingly at the berries as Bryn called them over to look at his little shelter.

"Right then, see the strong straight branches I've used to pitch the sides? Well, your staffs will do for two of them, but you'll need to find another five each, all about that length. I'll find the ones you'll need to make the central beam. Well then? What are you waiting for? The sooner you're done, the sooner we eat!"

They all shot off into the forest using their staffs to fight back against the undergrowth. Alfie was surprised at just how wild the forest was. In his own time it was much smaller and had many well-trodden paths. Here, it seemed so dense and full of rustlings and chirpings, as though wildlife was everywhere. There were lots of fallen branches lying amongst the undergrowth. Some had been there so long they were covered in moss and crumbled into pieces when he tried to pick them up, but there were fresh ones too. He snapped off some of the twigs to make them easier to carry back. It didn't take him long to find four.

Wandering further from the clearing, Alfie

spotted his fifth branch lying among a bed of ferns. He bent to pick it up and jumped as it was pulled from his hands. Amy's head poked through the ferns. She had her finger on her lips and indicated for him to crouch down beside her, pointing to something between the trees. Alfie's breath caught in his throat as he saw what she was pointing at. A stag. It stood tall, head raised, alerted by the rustling. Alfie crouched silently next to her. Reassured that the disturbance was nothing, the stag bowed its head and began to scrape its antlers against a tree.

"What's it doing?" Amy whispered in Alfie's ear.

"Rubbing the velvet from his horns," Alfie whispered back. He had never seen a stag in the wild before, but Robin had told him about the velvety covering on their antlers when they had found a discarded set in the woods.

"It's so beautiful," whispered Amy. They sat silently together, watching the magnificent creature. Alfie felt a warmth spreading through him as the worry over his lessons slipped away, and he sat quietly next to Amy, enjoying the moment. The stag raised its head and pricked up its ears as the silence was finally broken by loud rustling and raised voices. It turned and bolted away through the trees as Robin's voice cut clearly through the woods.

"Maddie! I told you, that one's too big – it's practically a whole tree!"

The moment lost, Alfie and Amy gathered their sticks and joined the twins on their way back to the clearing. Madeleine eventually gave up and dropped the huge log she was dragging behind her.

Bryn set to work creating two shelters. He bound a pair of branches together at the top so that they stood up like a triangle, then used them as a rest for one long branch which ran diagonally down to the ground. Alfie watched admiringly as the woodsman cut the sticks they had gathered to size and laid them against the central beam, binding them tight to create a pitched frame.

"Right then, get to work," said Bryn, nodding to a pile of leaves, fens and bracken as he started work on the second frame. Alfie grabbed handfuls of the materials the woodsman had gathered and began to cover the frame, weaving leafy twigs and ferns over the branches. The twins worked on the other side, squabbling as Madeleine told Robin he was working too slowly, and Robin argued that she was messing up his design. Alfie and Amy left them to it and moved over to the second shelter as Bryn finished building the frame. Bryn nodded approvingly and moved on to light a fire in the centre of the clearing and set up a frame for a pot he pulled out of his sack.

Alfie enjoyed weaving the shelter as he watched Bryn slicing up the mushrooms, greens and wild garlic and dropping them into the water that was beginning to bubble in the pot. He added some strips of dried meat from a pouch on his belt.

"Rabbit," he said as he saw Alfie watching. A delicious savoury smell wafted around the clearing, and Alfie took a deep sniff and gulped as his mouth began to water. He wondered what it would be like to live in the wild, gathering his own food and building his own shelters.

When they were finally finished roofing the shelter, Alfie and Amy spread out the blankets they had brought with them on the soft ground inside, removing all the stones that might poke through.

"Not bad," said Bryn, leaving the pot to bubble as he inspected their handiwork, adjusting the leaves and ferns here and there, and securing the twigs. "Not bad at all."

They all glowed at Bryn's approval. Alfie's

stomach growled loudly as they gathered around the fire. Bryn ladled large portions of the delicious stew into wooden bowls and pulled a large round loaf of bread from his sack and broke it into large chunks. The stew was delicious. Alfie enjoyed the meaty and squidgy textures of the different mushrooms and the strong flavours of the herbs and wild garlic against the chewy, spiced rabbit meat.

After their meal, they all tucked into the juicy berries Amy had collected, and Bryn began to tell them tales of Hexbridge and the surrounding villages. Some of them Alfie had already heard from his granny, such as the rumour that a giant prehistoric turtle lived in Archelon Lake, and stories of folks who had been led astray by enchanted waymarkers – standing stones placed to guide travellers that moved and guided the unwary from their paths until they became lost in the moors. However some of the things they heard were completely new to Alfie. Bryn told them that there was so much magic in the earth around Hexbridge that crops and farm animals fared better there than anywhere else in the world, and many residents over the years had developed strange abilities, such as magical healing powers, enhanced senses, shapeshifting, and even the ability to predict the future. Alfie wondered if anyone they knew had any of those abilities.

"I'm sure Granny has super senses," said Madeleine. "She always seems to know when I'm up to something."

"Phht! That's because you're always up to something," said Robin.

"What's that noise?" said Madeleine suddenly.

"It's a boar!" said Robin, jumping to his feet.

Bryn cupped his hands, raised them to his mouth and let out three owl-like hoots, two long and one short. By way of reply came three short hoots from the woods. Bryn beamed, got to his feet and strode across the clearing as Orin and Betsy emerged from the trees.

"You're early," said Bryn, leading Betsy to the stream as Orin sat down on a log near the fire and helped himself to a bowl of stew. "I didn't think we'd see you until the morning at least."

"There was nothing I could do there," said Orin, dunking a chunk of bread into his stew. "I have to get back to my books."

"The people I saw in my dream," said Amy, shuffling closer to the druid. "What's wrong with them?"

"They're weak. Very weak," said Orin. "It's as though almost all of their life has been sucked out of them."

"Will they die?" asked Alfie.

"Not if I can help it. But I need to do some reading. I haven't seen anything quite like this before. Amy, your dream – describe it to me again."

Alfie inched closer to the warmth of the fire as Amy recounted her nightmare of the creature made of shadows, fear and voices which fed on life and warmth, leaving black crosses in its wake. The flickering flames reflected in Madeleine and Robin's wide eyes as they listened.

"So the thing Amy saw was real?" asked Alfie. "Do you know what it was?"

Orin exchanged a glance with Bryn. "I have never seen one before, but I believe it is a wraith. A creature of darkness – of death. Something unnatural that should never have been brought into this world."

"What does it want?" asked Robin.

"For itself – nothing," said the druid. "A wraith is summoned and bound to a single goal set by its master."

"Summoned?" said Alfie. "Where from?"

"A wraith is a soul of the departed, dragged back

into this world by dark magic and the blood of its master. It is bound to do the task it was given in the summoning and cannot return to its rest until it succeeds. As it is dead, it is drawn to the living and must borrow life from them until it can leave this plane."

"So that's what it did to those people – it fed on their life?" said Robin. The druid nodded.

Alfie shuddered involuntarily as he remembered his own magic urging him to take the life of the hare. Orin had told him that magic is neither bad or good, only the person who wields it, but right now it felt more frightening than ever to possess something that consumes life itself.

"This wraith, you said it *borrowed* life. So if we found it and sent it back to where it came from, would those people recover?"

"I'm not sure it's that simple," said Orin. "Amy, you said that you heard many voices calling out from inside this creature."

"Yes. Dozens of them, all cold and frightened."

"This is a dark spell indeed," said Orin, the flames casting shadows on to his face as he stoked the fire. "I've only ever heard of single spirits being raised from the grave, but this wraith is different. It consists of many souls, all of whom suffered the same cruel death."

"The black crosses drawn on the doors," Alfie croaked.

Orin nodded grimly. "This wraith was raised from a plague pit."

Alfie stared at him in silence. All those people who had died such a terrible death, dragged back into this world against their will. What kind of person would do such a thing?

"It seemed to be searching for something," said Amy, pulling her cloak around her shoulders. "It could sense it, but couldn't quite find it."

Orin sat quietly watching the flames as Bryn handed round the berries. Alfie sensed there was something they weren't being told.

"You know, don't you?" said Alfie. "You know who summoned the wraith, and why?"

"I have my suspicions," said Orin. "I have only known one person who could be so selfish, so single-minded, so prepared to employ dark forces with no thought for those caught in their wake."

A name crept into Alfie's head. A name he had read in Orin's first letter to him. The person responsible for forcing Orin to hide the ancient magic inside Alfie.

"Agrodonn?" he whispered. "The druid that

went bad and tried to take the magic from you?"

"Agrodonn," said the druid.

Alfie remembered vividly the tales the druid had told him of how Agrodonn had brought famine, disease and destruction on the villages all around in order to get Orin to give up the magic Alfie now guarded.

"But you told Alfie he was gone, that he wasn't a threat any more!" said Amy, red berry juice trickling through her fingers as she clenched her fists.

"I stripped his powers from him and he hasn't been seen in many years," said Orin. "I assumed that he had given up."

Alfie's stomach tightened. "So, if he's back, he can only be after one thing." He gripped the protective talisman around his neck. "The magic. Inside me."

Orin sighed deeply. "I fear that I will forever be asking your forgiveness for burdening you with it."

Alfie could hardly believe it. He had only known about the magic inside him since he had received the talisman and Orin's castle barely a year ago, and this was the third time the druid's legacy had hurt others around him. But perhaps it didn't always have to bring misfortune. . .

"Could I use the magic to help the people the wraith has fed on?" he asked the druid. "I could drain the energy from plants, from flames, and use it to heal them."

"You should not use the magic at all while the wraith is searching for it," said Orin. "But you could not help them anyway. They cannot be healed until their *own* life force is returned. I must search my books now to find a way to do this."

"Agrodonn – if he summoned the wraith, where is he now?" asked Alfie.

"Hiding, like a coward, I'll bet!" grunted Bryn.

"He'll be waiting for the wraith to find the magic before he comes out of hiding, but I'm sure we'll see him before this is over."

He stood up and took Betsy's reins.

"Should we come with you?" asked Alfie, glancing around at the others. None of them looked particularly keen to stay out in the woods with the wraith roaming the land.

"You'll be safer here," said Orin. "If it comes this way your talisman will hide the magic from it. It is more likely to come to the castle and the island in the lake as those are places where you used the magic, and its vibrations will still be lingering.

Alfie. . ." He sighed deeply. "Once again, I'm sorry for putting you at risk. You must travel home until this threat has passed."

"How?" asked Alfie. "You said the potion everyone took would stop them from travelling back."

You alone could manage it, but it would be wise for you all to arrive home together. I will brew up a potion to counteract the effects." He led Betsy across the clearing. "It will take a little time to prepare. Return to the castle in the morning and I will send you home."

The woods seemed darker and colder as Orin disappeared into the trees. Bryn tried to lighten the mood with more stories and bad jokes, but Alfie could see how uneasy everyone in the group seemed. He noticed them all glancing at him out of the corner of their eyes as they listened to Bryn. They were worried about him. He made a brave effort to laugh and join in Bryn's jokes to show that he wasn't afraid. But deep down he felt his insides turning to ice.

Alfie and Robin talked in low whispers for a while as the group all settled down to sleep. Soon the only noise was the crackling of the fire, Bryn's rumbling snores, and the distant hooting of owls.

Alfie lay awake thinking long after Robin fell asleep. If Orin was right about Agrodonn raising the wraith, the sooner they went home the better. Finally he fell into an uneasy slumber.

Several hours later the forest fell silent as a shadow flowed between the trees. It stopped once, as though sensing something nearby, then continued towards its goal.

8

The Black Cross

The dawn bird chorus woke Alfie early the next
morning. The twins were already up and sharing
out the last of the loaves Bryn had brought with
them. Amy was still asleep and the woodsman
was nowhere to be seen. Everything seemed better
in the light of day with the sound of the twins
squabbling over who was going to wash last night's
bowls in the stream and the birds filling the forest
with song.

"Thanks, Robin," he said as his cousin handed
him a flagon. He took a long draught, enjoying the
cool, fresh stream water. Amy was still sprawled
out under her cloak in the other shelter, a little

drool running from the corner of her mouth and her hair sticking out at odd angles. He grinned and crept towards her with the flagon of water, finger pressed to his lips so that his cousins wouldn't say a word. Standing above her, he tipped the flagon so that a thin stream of water poured down on to the back of her neck. He leapt out of the way as she woke with a yell and jumped to her feet.

"You are SO dead, Bloomers!" she yelled, putting her head down and charging at him like a bull. Alfie leapt nimbly out of her way, only to slip on the mossy rocks. Amy saw her opportunity and swept his legs out from under him, sending him splashing down into the stream.

"You totally deserved that," laughed Madeleine, grasping his arm and dragging him up out of the water.

"Yeah, I did," grinned Alfie, his teeth chattering as Amy tipped the rest of the flagon over his head, just to make sure he was completely drenched.

"I see everyone's up and bathed," laughed Bryn, appearing from between the trees. He heated a pat of butter in a pan and proceeded to scramble a dozen eggs he had collected.

"Woodland hens lay the best eggs," he said as

they scooped up the scrambled eggs with hunks of bread and munched away.

Everyone was keen to get back to the castle to hear how Orin's research was going, so they packed up quickly and put out the fire with stream water as soon as they had finished eating.

"Leave the shelters," said Bryn. "I'll take them down later."

Alfie felt sad as they hurried back through the forest. He had been looking forward to two weeks in the past learning from the druid, but they were returning after only a few days. Would he even get the chance to come back? Maybe he could never return as long as Agrodonn was still at large.

The village was quiet as they passed through.

"We must be up before everyone," said Madeleine. But Alfie felt a growing sense of unease and knew that the others did too.

"John!" Bryn called to the only person they saw.

"Bryn," nodded the man, stopping work on the fence he was mending.

"Where is everyone?"

"Off searching for the animals that escaped last night. Something must have put the frights up them – they burst straight through the fences. Don't suppose you've seen my horses, or sheep?"

"Sorry," said Bryn, grim-faced. "I'll round up any I see."

No one said anything, but Alfie could only think of one thing that could have frightened the animals so much.

"Alfie," said Amy, gripping his arm. "I had another dream last night. I forgot about it after you woke me up like that. I don't remember much, just that the castle was in it, and Orin and Ashford."

Alfie looked up at the castle's chimneys; there was no smoke rising from any of them. He clenched the talisman around his neck like a lucky charm as they raced up the hill. Amy was leading the way and she stopped dead as she reached the top, staring across the moat.

"What is it?" asked Robin. "Is the drawbridge up?" Amy didn't answer. Alfie stepped around her and his heart skipped painfully in his chest. Scored across the underside of the raised drawbridge was a mark. A black cross.

"No!" cried Madeleine.

"How do we get in?" Alfie asked, grabbing Bryn's woollen waistcoat as he stood staring in horror at the black mark. Alfie tried shaking the huge figure, but he was as immovable as a mountain. "Bryn, is there another way in?" he shouted, pummelling the woodsman's chest. Robin was staring, ashen-faced, as Madeleine and Amy frantically looked for a way to open the drawbridge.

"Right, yes … the drawbridge," said Bryn, snapping back to life. He flung himself on to the ground by the moat and reached down into the fast-flowing water. "Where is it, where is it…" he muttered as he shuffled along on his stomach, searching for something in the wall of the moat below the surface of the water. "Aha," he said suddenly. Alfie peered over the edge of the moat and saw Bryn had seized a small handle set into the rocky bank. He gave it a tug. Instantly a loud clanking began and the drawbridge started to lower, all too slowly, towards them. Alfie couldn't wait for it to drop. He clambered up on to it, racing across as it thumped down into position and the portcullis rattled up into the gate-tower.

The others followed Alfie as he ran into the courtyard.

"Orin… Ashford!" he yelled, echoed by Madeleine and Bryn. The courtyard was eerily silent. He flung open the door and ran through the castle shouting, cold dread building as he darted through empty rooms.

"The library!" shouted Robin, running up the

stairs. Alfie overtook him on the second flight, barrelled along the corridor and burst into the library. It was empty, but the entrance to the study was open. Fearful of what he might find, Alfie crept towards the door.

"Orin?" he whispered, tiptoeing through the little passage and into the study. The druid was sitting in a chair with his back to them, every surface around him covered in books. He was slumped forwards, head resting on a pile of papers on his desk on to which a guttering candle was dripping wax.

"He's been working all night," said Robin. "Maybe he fell asleep?"

Alfie could tell that even Robin didn't believe his own words. One of Orin's arms hung down by his side. Ink dripped from his fingers on to the scattered papers below. Bryn rushed over to the druid and shook him by the shoulders until his limp body slid out of the chair. Bryn caught him and Alfie hurried over to help carry him to the armchair in front of the fire. Alfie tried not to think about how cold Orin felt.

"Al, he ... he's not dead ... is he?" asked Amy, keeping her distance. Alfie hardly dared to breathe as Madeleine bent to take Orin's pulse. Dropping his wrist she put her ear to his chest. She frowned and Alfie's own heart almost stopped beating as she grabbed a silver spoon and held it under the druid's nose, checking for steam from his breath. Alfie gripped Amy's arm as Madeleine sighed, took a torch from her pocket and shone the light into each of Orin's eyes. Finally the tiniest of smiles crept across her face.

"He's alive."

The whole group took a collective breath and sank down on to chairs and rugs, shaking with relief.

"He might be alive, but only just," said Madeleine. "He's barely breathing. And his heartbeat is so faint."

"That thing ... the wraith," bellowed Bryn, jumping to his feet. "It did this to him! He had his back to it when it floated in here and drained the life from him! He didn't even have a chance to defend himself! I'll find that thing... I'll track it down, and when I do..." He pounded his fist into his palm as Madeleine and Amy guided him to a chair.

"Robin, brew some tea," said Madeleine. "Use that jar labelled mugwort and camomile – add some valerian too. I think we could all use some."

Alfie looked around the room as Robin brewed the calming tea and Madeleine and Amy comforted Bryn. Nothing appeared to have been disturbed other than an overturned ink bottle on the druid's desk. The wraith really had caught Orin unawares. He clenched his fists at the cowardice of the man who had sent it. If the druid was right, the wraith had been searching for him, Alfie – for his magic – and had taken Orin instead. Had it found Ashford too?

Running to Ashford's bedroom, he threw open the door without knocking. Ashford was lying under the covers, a book resting on his chest. For a brief moment Alfie thought he was sleeping.

"Ashford?" he whispered as he reached out and shook his shoulder. There was no response. He wasn't going to wake up.

Alfie suddenly felt as though the whole room was closing in on him. He staggered dizzily to the window. Orin and Ashford had been taken by the wraith. What if it returned for him too? He had to do something, but what?

He stood by the window, taking slow, deep breaths as Orin had taught him, trying to calm his churning stomach and thudding heart. He gazed at the hills, and watched the clouds scudding across the sky as he willed himself to calm down. Finally the cold, clammy grip of fear began to leave him as he watched the birds circling overhead. *The birds! That was it!* He bolted from the room, heading for the stairs to the nearest tower. His hair was swept back by the breeze as he stepped out on to the top of the tower and spun around, searching. He finally saw what he was looking for: a raven perched down on the lower battlements, pecking at insects trying to hide in the cracks in the stone.

"Hey! Hey . . . Mr Raven!" he shouted, waving his arms about his head. The raven stopped what it was doing and cocked its head to peer up at him, as though wondering whether this strange boy was worth its attention. "Please, if you don't mind, I have a message to send. A message for Muninn and Bone." He kept on waving and shouting until the raven finally seemed to decide that he was interesting enough to pay some attention to. It launched itself from the wall and, with a few flaps of its powerful wings, it landed on the wall in front of Alfie, who jumped back in surprise at the size of the bird and its powerful beak up close.

"Hi, er, Mr Raven, sir," said Alfie, showing extra respect just in case the raven was an aloof shapeshifter, just like Caspian Bone. Caspian once told him that if he ever needed to get a message to him, he just needed to tell a raven. Well, this one seemed to be listening...

"Please, could you take a message to Caspian Bone for me?" The bird ruffled its feathers and gave a little shuffle, which Alfie decided must mean yes. "There's something out here," said Alfie. "A wraith. We think it's after my magic. It drained the life from Orin and Ashford. We don't know what to do – we need Caspian's help." The bird was still staring at him. Alfie began to feel silly. "Um, did you understand any of that?" he asked sheepishly. Alfie knew birds didn't roll their eyes, but this one gave a very good imitation of the gesture as it cawed three times and launched itself from the tower to flap away into the sky.

The others were seated silently around Orin when he returned to the study.

"It got Ashford too," he told them. The colour drained from their already pale faces. Bryn got to his feet.

"You've got to leave here," he said, pacing the room. "Orin wanted you to go today – you can't stay while this *thing* is around."

"We can't go back," said Robin. "We drank that potion, and it looks as though Orin didn't have time to brew the one that would let us travel home."

"Madeleine could brew the counter potion, if we can find the recipe," said Bryn.

"She probably could," said Alfie, "but how would things change in our future if we left now? Do we leave Ashford here with you and Orin? What if it comes back for you? What if . . . what if they die? It could change everything in the future we'd be travelling back to, and we might not be able to come back and help you. No – we can't go back. We need to stay and find a way to fix this and banish the wraith."

"But how, Al?" said Amy. "Even Orin had to come back here to research what it is and how to cure the people it hurt. How can we take it on ourselves?"

"Maybe we won't have to," said Alfie. "I just sent a message to Caspian. I bet he'll be able to help us."

"Maybe Orin found something that can help us too," said Robin. "I'll have a look." He hurried over to the books and notes strewn over Orin's desk and began to search through them. Alfie suspected it was so that he didn't have to sit looking at Orin slumped in his armchair, eyes blank and staring. Madeleine got up and placed a blanket over him, closed his eyelids and turned his face away from them. Alfie felt a wave of gratitude to her. Now it just looked as though the druid was sleeping. He was always amazed at Madeleine's complete lack of unease around blood and sickness. He took a gulp of the soothing tea that Robin had left for him and tried to turn his mind from the horrible possibilities floating around his head.

A cry from Robin made them all look up. He had picked up the ink-splattered papers from the floor and was staring at one of them.

"What is it, Rob?" asked Amy.

"Take a look," said Robin, holding the page out before them. Alfie stared at the scrawl on the page. Orin had used the last of his strength to write a message with his finger in the spilt ink:

Witch
Demon
Ro

"Witch Demon Ro?" repeated Madeleine. "What does that mean? Maybe he thought the wraith was a witch, or..." She paused, "A demon."

"No, I don't think that's it." Alfie chewed his thumbnail as he tried to make sense of the message. "Look at the way his finger trailed ink down the page after the 'o', I think he lost consciousness before he finished writing."

"Why do *Demon* and *Ro* have capital letters?" asked Robin. "Maybe it's a place name? But it's not one I've ever heard of."

There was a crash as Bryn leapt to his feet, sending his chair toppling. "The witch!" he shouted. "He wants us to fetch the witch!"

"What witch?" asked Alfie, startled by the sudden explosion from Bryn.

"The Witch of Demon Rock!" said Bryn, "She may be more powerful than even Orin himself, though she knows more about the dark side of magic than anyone should." He began to pace the room. "I don't like it, but if that's what Orin wanted, that's what we must do. If anyone can help him, she can!"

"Where is this Demon Rock?" asked Alfie, unsure about the sound of the place, or the witch.

"About sixty miles northeast of here. It's one of several islands – there are monks living on some of them, but not on her island."

"I know those islands," said Madeleine. "They're near Bamburgh Castle. We sailed out to them on a school trip, didn't we, Robin?"

"There were so many seabirds," said Robin,

almost wistfully. "Demon Rock was the really craggy one with the tall pillars of rock in the sea around it. It was covered in puffins. I don't see how anyone could live there though."

"That's the one," said Bryn. "If we leave soon we should get there by dusk. We'll hire a boat to row out to the island the next morning."

"Shouldn't we wait for a reply from Caspian first?" asked Alfie as Bryn marched towards the door.

"There's still time," said Bryn. "I'll need to pack some food and water, borrow a cart from the village, then saddle up the horses." His face suddenly dropped and he rushed from the room. Alfie and the others hurried after him, wondering what had upset him as he thundered down the stairs and out into the courtyard.

"Betsy! BETSY!" he yelled, running towards the stable. Alfie could already see that it was no use shouting. Lying in the straw as near lifeless as Orin and Ashford was Bryn's horse. "Oh, Betsy!" said Bryn, stroking her long nose. Nearby lay Orin's horse, and Wesley the goat, whose mouth still clamped around a sweatshirt of Amy's he was chewing on when the wraith had arrived. The only creatures who didn't seemed to be affected were the chickens, but they were silently cowering in their roosts, afraid to venture out.

"I'm sorry, Bryn," said Alfie, putting his hand on the big man's shoulder. "But if we can get help for Orin, we can make her better too. Maybe Caspian can help us." As if to answer him there was a loud cawing from above as a raven swooped down into the courtyard. It perched on a post near the stable and bobbed impatiently, its shoulders hunched. A small black glass vial dangled from a thread around its neck. It bobbed its head again and Alfie removed the vial.

"Did you speak to Caspian?" he asked. "Is he coming?" The raven shook its feathers and a strange change came over it. It straightened up and raised its beak in an arrogant fashion as its eyes turned milky white. It opened its beak, but instead of a raven's caw, a deep, male human voice came from its throat.

"This is Muninn," it snapped. "What do you want?"

Alfie looked from the twins to Amy as they all stared at the raven.

"Isn't Muninn Caspian's business partner?" whispered Robin. "I think he's speaking through the raven."

"You waste time with the obvious, boy!" said the

raven. "What do you want?"

"We were hoping to speak to Caspian," said Alfie, staring at the raven. If this was Caspian's business partner he was very glad he wasn't meeting him face to face. His voice was terrifying enough.

"Caspian is away on business. He will not return for three days. WHAT DO YOU WANT?"

"Your help, we want your help," stammered Alfie. "A wraith drained the life from Orin and Ashford, it's after the magic Orin gave me. Can you help us?"

"Orin is Caspian's client," said the raven. "Caspian will deal with the matter on his return. You will go home now. Take three drops each from the vial around my messenger's neck. It will enable you all to travel forward to your time."

Alfie looked down at the vial in his hand then stared back at the raven. "So that's it? You're sending us home? You're not going to help?" he asked incredulously.

"You are Caspian's clients. He will deal with the matter on his return," repeated Muninn.

"That's not how solicitors work," said Robin, waving his finger angrily at the raven. It was a picture that, at any other time, Alfie would have found comical, but not today. "Orin is a client of the firm, not just Caspian, and Alfie is too. You *have* to help them."

The raven stretched upwards and spread its wings threateningly. "I take orders from no one – especially children," it spat. "I have helped you enough. You *will* return home."

Alfie had noticed Bryn's face getting redder and redder as he listened to the raven. Finally he snapped.

"Why, you straggly little crow!" he bellowed, charging at the bird. The milky colour faded from the raven's eyes. It shook itself and became much more birdlike as it screeched at Bryn and flapped away from his grasp and up over the castle walls.

"I'm sorry," Bryn panted as Alfie stared forlornly after the raven. "It got me so mad. I didn't mean to drive it away."

"It's fine," said Alfie, sinking to the cobbles. "We wouldn't have been able to reason with him. He wasn't going to help us."

"Man, and I thought Caspian was arrogant!" said Amy, miming swinging a baseball bat at the spot where the raven had been perched.

"No wonder Emily Fortune is scared of him," said Madeleine. "Who'd want to work for *that*?"

Alfie noticed Robin was chewing his lip as he

always did when considering something he didn't like.

"What are you thinking, Robin?" asked Alfie.

"Maybe he's right," said Robin. "Maybe we should go home."

"Are you kidding me?" cried Madeleine, stepping in front of him, a spot of red appearing on each of her cheeks. "You think we should just head home and leave Orin and Betsy, and all those people in Miggleswick? While that … that *thing* Amy saw is still floating around here?" She jabbed him with her finger. "I'M not going *anywhere*."

Alfie edged between them before Madeleine built herself up into too much of a rage.

"Think about it," said Robin. "The wraith is after Alfie's magic, so it makes sense for us to leave. Muninn said that Caspian will deal with this when he gets back. We don't know anything about this stuff, so maybe we *should* leave this to them. There's nothing much we can do ourselves, is there?"

"What about the witch?" asked Alfie. "We could still go and see her."

"It would be a long trip without horses," said Bryn. "Two days. If we left now we might make it for nightfall tomorrow, but we'd need to wait for the morning to row out there, and all that time the wraith will be searching for Alfie. Maybe Robin and the crow are right. You get yourselves home and I'll go to Demon Rock and speak to the witch."

"Al's the one in most danger if we stay," said Amy at last. "He should decide."

Alfie's head was beginning to whirl again. He didn't want to leave Orin and Ashford, but he didn't want to risk Amy or his cousins being attacked by the wraith. But if he went home without knowing what would happen to Orin, would his future be very different? If Orin died and he didn't inherit the castle, would he even remember he had been back here in the past? His temple began to throb as he tried to understand how time travel might affect everything. What should he do? Everyone was staring at him expectantly. Finally his thoughts seemed to click into place. He couldn't risk losing Orin and Ashford. He turned back to the group.

"We're staying," he said firmly.

Madeleine smiled and even Robin nodded in agreement. Amy patted him on the back.

"We're with you, Al."

Only Bryn didn't look happy.

"I understand the loyalty you feel to Orin," he

said. "But if the wraith comes for us, I don't know if I can protect you all against it."

"Who needs protecting?" said Madeleine. "We can look after ourselves."

"Yes," said Alfie. "And with the dreams Amy has been having, maybe she'll be able to warn us if it's coming. We're going with you."

Bryn seemed about to argue, but then looked down at Alfie's set and determined face. "I don't have a choice in this do I?" he asked.

"Nope!" said Amy. "So let's get a move on, shall we?"

9

The Journey North

By eleven o' clock they had packed up everything they needed to take with them. Sparky had zipped out the second Alfie and Robin had opened the wardrobe in their room to change clothes. They wasted ten minutes trying to catch the little silver bird as it chirped its way around the room in a game of hide-and-seek that it seemed to find great fun. Alfie finally gave up.

"Well then, you'll just have to stay there, wherever you are," he shouted to the room in general before grabbing their bags and closing the door. He shook his head at Robin. "Out of *everything* the elf queen did when she invaded the castle, bringing that bird to life has to be the most annoying!"

Bryn had filled a small sack with bread, cheese and fruits and handed Alfie and Robin filled water-skins as they joined him outside, locking the castle door behind them.

"This is great," said Madeleine, hanging hers from her belt. "No plastic and it just rolls up when it's empty. I'll take one of these home with me."

Robin nudged Alfie. "I thought I'd wait until the girls are drinking out of them before I tell them they're made from cows' bladders," he grinned.

"Aw cute, you're trying to gross out the ickle girlies," said Amy, popping her chin on his shoulder and ruffling his hair. "It's actually a sheep's bladder. Bryn told us." She strolled away whistling to join Madeleine, who was helping Bryn make sure Betsey and Wesley were left in comfortable positions in the straw.

Alfie felt a pang of guilt at leaving Orin and Ashford as they left the castle and Bryn pulled the hidden handle to raise the drawbridge. He knew there was nothing else that could happen to them, even if the wraith did come back, but it seemed strange to just leave them helpless.

"Hold on," he said under his breath, before following the others down the hill. "We'll be back soon."

"Why can't we carry our bows?" asked Madeleine as they hurried after Bryn, each taking two steps to match one of the woodsman's strides. He had made the twins bundle their bows and quiver of arrows into a sack and had warned them not to carry them out in the open.

"Orin has an agreement with the king. He is the warden of the forest around Hexbridge, and we are safe there, but once we head into the king's forest, well ... that's a different matter! The last thing you want is to be accused of poaching; even eating berries or using fallen wood as we did yesterday in Orin's forest would have us pilloried if we did the same elsewhere."

"Pilloried?" repeated Amy.

"A wooden frame that traps your head and hands," explained Robin. "People think they're called stocks, but those are the ones that trap your legs."

"Oh, I've seen those in films," said Madeleine. "People throw rotten eggs and vegetables at you."

"Only if you're lucky," said Bryn ominously. "I've seen them throw much worse."

They made good time that morning. Alfie noticed Bryn was leading them on a well-trodden route through the trees in his haste to cover as much distance as possible before nightfall. Despite the cool shelter of the trees, Alfie soon felt hot and sticky. He had refilled his water-skin twice in the streams they passed before Bryn finally stopped in the early afternoon.

"We're passing out of Orin's forest now," he said as they sat in the shade of the trees at the edge of the forest and he handed out food to the group. "We need to be careful from here on out. Don't talk to anyone if you can help it, and stick to the names I gave you. Do you remember them?" He called out the names one by one and they raised their hands in turn.

"Alfred, Robert, Amery ... Maud."

Alfie noted that Madeleine hardly grimaced at all when she raised her hand at the last name.

Alfie finished off his meal of bread and cheese with an apple, leaving the core for a red squirrel Robin had pointed out watching them from the branches above.

"Ready?" said Bryn. "It's eighteen miles until the forest where we'll spend the night. Folks don't travel much between villages, so we'll keep to the trees, hills and moors wherever we can to avoid attention."

Alfie was glad to be out of the forest and back in the daylight for a while as they tramped across the moors, following the tiny runs the hares had created through the heather. Every now and then one of them sprang out in front of the group, stared at them for a startled moment, then bounded swiftly away, white tail bobbing. Robin pointed out birds flying overhead, naming kites, falcons and pheasants.

The heather kept catching on Alfie's woollen trousers and he was surprised to see Madeleine striding ahead just behind Bryn, skirts hitched up into her belt. He was amazed that she seemed oblivious to the scratchy heather. Then a splash of blue as she walked revealed her secret.

"Maddie! You're wearing jeans?" he called after her. They all hurried up to join her as she quickly lowered her skirts.

"Oh no you don't!" said Amy, yanking Madeleine's skirts back up to reveal her jeans. "So we have to wear these itchy trousers and get scratched legs while you wear your jeans?"

Madeleine grinned. "Orin said I had to wear the dress. He didn't say I couldn't wear these under it."

"You can't wear those," said Robin. "You'll give us away."

"To who?" said Madeleine, waving her arms to indicate the empty moors. "The hares? The birds? I walk quicker with them and I'm keeping them on. If we see anyone coming I'll cover them."

Alfie put his hand over his face and shook his head as Robin started to argue.

"HUSH!" he bellowed, startling a family of grouse, which flapped away noisily. "Maddie, wear the jeans if you must, but for Orin's sake, let's keep walking!"

Madeleine hitched up her skirts again and hurried happily ahead after Bryn.

After another hour of walking they made their way down to grassland. Alfie figured they had walked about ten miles since they had set out from the castle and his feet were hurting. The medieval boots he was wearing were well made, but they didn't cushion his feet nearly as much as his own walking shoes and trainers. It would be another twelve miles before they reached the forest Bryn was leading them to – hours of walking. He wasn't sure how long he could keep going. He doubted Bryn had considered their much shorter legs when he worked out how long the journey would take, but with the wraith behind them they couldn't afford to slow down.

As the moors sloped down the heather became less of a problem, but the land became more marshy and Alfie could feel water starting to soak through his boots as they squidged slowly onwards.

Bryn seemed to have realized the group was tiring. He kept calling out encouragement and stopping regularly, but Alfie could tell that he was trying not to get annoyed at their slow progress. He kept trying to pick up the pace, but his feet were hurting a lot now and the marsh was slowing them all down.

They stopped at a cluster of rocks to sit and drink the last of their water. As they got up to leave, Bryn seemed to spy something in the distance and perked up.

"Stay there," he said, hurrying towards the dirt track beyond the line of trees.

"What did he see?" asked Robin. "Are we supposed to hide?"

Alfie listened carefully and heard the gentle clopping of horses' hooves and the rumble of wheels.

"Ho there!" he heard Bryn call. He could hear him talking to someone, but couldn't hear what they were saying. They seemed to be negotiating something.

"Lads! Lass!" Bryn called at last.

"I guess he wants us to go over there," said Alfie, getting up and hurrying through the trees and bushes towards the track. Bryn was standing by a cart, pulled by the biggest horse Alfie had ever seen.

"She's a beauty, isn't she?" said Bryn, patting the horse on the neck.

"She is indeed," said the wizened old man sitting at the front of the cart, holding the reins. He gave them a wide and gummy grin as Alfie tried not to stare at the gigantic wart on the end of his nose. Alfie gave a little bow, as did Robin and Amy. Madeleine dropped an extremely quick curtsey.

"We're in luck! Barnabas here is on his way home from delivering grain to the village yonder. He lives about thirteen miles north in a village up by the king's forest and has agreed to take us that far."

Alfie could have leapt up on to the cart and hugged Barnabas as the others all cheered.

Barnabas gave a loud meaningful cough and held out his hand.

"Oh, of course," said Bryn. "Maud, get over here.

I've told Barnabas you've been training with the great druid down in Hexbridge. I promised him some of that magic ointment of yours for his, well, for his. . ." He tapped the side of his nose.

"Oh!" said Madeleine, as if she'd only just seen the wart that was big enough to be a second nose. She rummaged in her pocket for the little jar and held it out. "Here it is, sir."

"Well, put it on for him, lass!" said Bryn.

"Of course, Uncle," growled Madeleine as Barnabas hopped down from the cart. Alfie was always impressed with how well Madeleine dealt with even the deepest cuts, but she couldn't hide her grimace as she spread a thick dollop of the green ointment onto the huge wart. "All done," she said, pocketing the jar and wiping her fingers on her skirts.

"There ain't no magic words or nothing?" said Barnabas, sounding rather disappointed.

"Go on, sis, say the magic words," grinned Robin.

Alfie took pity on Madeleine as she fumbled around for some magical-sounding words.

"Here, let me," he said, stepping forwards and waving his hand around the old man's nose. In his most impressive voice he began to recite:

"'Twas brillig, and the slithy toves
Did gyre and gimble in the wabe:
All mimsy were the borogoves,
And the mome raths outgrabe."

Alfie could see the others trying not to laugh as Barnabas looked suitably impressed with Alfie's spell.

"Much obliged," he said, and nodded. "I can feel it shrinking already. Now, hop in the back. I'll have you there before dusk."

"What was that?" asked Bryn as they all clambered into the back of the cart. "I haven't heard Orin use words like that before."

"'The Jabberwocky'." Alfie grinned as the others snorted with laughter. "A poem I learnt at school."

"Ah well," shrugged Bryn. "It made him feel better; that's half the magic. And if that ointment of Madeleine's is even half as good as Orin's it should help with that wart. While we're thinking of it, you should put some on your feet too."

As the cart rumbled back on its journey, everyone pulled their shoes off with gasps of relief and began to rub the ointment into their chaffed heels and toes. Alfie was amazed at how it instantly soothed his aching feet. Madeleine really was a marvel at herbology and healing. Alfie pushed down the little spark of jealousy that started to ignite again in his chest. It wasn't Madeleine's fault that he couldn't tell the difference between many different herbs, or Robin's fault that he still couldn't make head nor tail of even the simplest incantations. His magic had just been given to him; they had learnt all of this, almost on their own. He wondered if Orin would be disappointed in his ability to learn everything that came with being a druid's apprentice.

Bryn hopped up into the front with the old man, and Alfie stretched out in the back of the cart, head on a sack of straw, Amy and the twins at either side of him.

"Not quite the holiday we expected, eh, Al?" said Amy as they stared up at the sky.

"Not exactly," sighed Alfie, following the flight of a hawk against the grey-tinged clouds. "Sorry I got you all mixed up in this ... again."

"Will you just quit it with the apologizing?" said Madeleine. "We're here because we wanted to be. We *stayed* because we wanted to."

"She's right," said Robin. "Stop holding yourself responsible for everyone else. You don't have to carry the world on your shoulders all the time."

"Exactly," said Amy, stifling a yawn. "You've got us to help carry it."

Alfie smiled to himself as Amy's yawn set the others off. One by one they closed their eyes and drifted off to sleep as the rocking cart carried them onwards, closer to Demon Rock. As his eyelids began to droop, Alfie wondered what they would find there. He didn't believe storybook tales of evil witches, and knew that most of the people burned at the stake in years to come were just poor old women who had run foul of their superstitious neighbours. Orin had directed them to the witch, so surely she wouldn't be someone to be wary of, would she? Still, the rocky island didn't sound very hospitable sitting out in the cold North Sea with the waves crashing over it. What sort of person would live there? As the rumble of the cart turned into the rumbling and crashing of waves in his mind, Alfie drifted off to sleep.

It seemed only minutes before Bryn was shaking his shoulder.

"Alfred. Wake up lad!"

Alfie blinked himself awake. The sun had slipped lower in the sky and there was a bit of a chill in the air, but there was still daylight left. Amy and the twins were already stretching and pulling on their shoes. Alfie pulled his on quickly, noticing how much the ointment had eased his feet. He jumped down from the cart and thanked Will, who seemed very happy indeed. The wart on his nose had already begun to shrink. Madeleine applied another dose of ointment, with barely a grimace this time, and they bade him goodbye.

"Good man, that," said Bryn, waving as the cart trundled down into the village. "Asks few questions and took us even further than I expected." He nodded towards the forest bordering the track. "Another five miles through there and we'll be nearly halfway."

"Only halfway?" groaned Amy. "I knew we should have brought Artan!"

"Who's Artan?" asked Bryn.

"A friend," said Alfie, stepping on Amy's foot while the twins glared at her. "He ... er ... has a very fast cart. He could have got us there in no time."

"In that case, I wish you'd brought him too," sighed Bryn. "The weather's turning and I don't think we'll have as much luck hitching a ride tomorrow. There's no way we'll reach the coast by tomorrow evening if we walk as slowly as today. If only we had the money to hire a cart and horses ourselves!"

At that moment a woman came bustling along with a baby strapped to her back and a basket of firewood under her arm. She stopped and stared at the group as though they were aliens. Alfie quickly checked to see if Madeleine's jeans were showing, but the woman just seemed astounded to see strangers.

"Afternoon, mistress," said Bryn, nodding to her. She seemed startled to hear him speak and bobbed a quick curtsey before hurrying away, casting suspicious looks back at them.

"Into the forest," said Bryn, hurrying them towards the trees. "As I said, few folks travel and we could do without the attention strangers bring."

This forest felt different. Alfie wasn't sure if it was the time of day, the worry he felt, or because Hexbridge Forest felt safer because it was close to home, but there seemed to be something foreboding about this one. The tall, dark trees were closer together, and the canopies blocked out much of the remaining daylight. The only benefit was that there wasn't much undergrowth to battle their way through, making trekking through the trees easier. Still, he wasn't looking forward to the prospect of sleeping in there, especially with the wraith searching for them, and Agrodonn lurking somewhere until it completed its task. He knew they had to succeed in their own quest if there was to be any chance of stopping them. He hoped they'd put enough distance between themselves and the wraith, but with no way of knowing where it was, he felt as though it could be lurking in the shadows of any of the trees around them.

"Bit grim, isn't it?" said Amy, falling in step with Alfie as they pushed on through the woods. "Look, sorry about mentioning Artan," she whispered. "Totally forgot. Won't happen again."

"Apology accepted," said Alfie. "I'm just worried because Caspian said we need to be careful about what we say while we're here."

"Understood," said Amy. "But understand this: you stand on my foot again, and I'll drop you in another stream. OK?"

The air became colder as they trudged further through the forest. Alfie's feet felt better, but his legs were really starting to ache and the woollen trousers were starting to make his skin feel sore. He didn't dare to ask Bryn if they could take even a brief rest. Their slow pace had already delayed the woodsman in getting help for Orin. Again he wondered if they shouldn't have just gone home as Muninn had demanded.

Bryn stopped suddenly and crouched down. Alfie looked over his shoulder and saw something lying in his path. The woolly carcass of a sheep.

"The swines!" Bryn roared.

"What killed it?" asked Robin.

"Not what, who!" said Bryn. "It's a trap. A trap set for wolves, or any other animal that might feed on it!" Alfie, Amy and the twins covered their noses with their cloaks as Bryn reached into the open stomach of the sheep and pulled out a handful of dark green leaves with oddly shaped purple flowers. "Wolf's bane," he growled.

"That's deadly poison!" cried Madeleine. "Who would set a trap like that?"

"The wardens and rangers of the king's forest are not always honourable men," said Bryn. He raked out a hole in the soil and buried the poisonous leaves, placing a few rocks on top of the spot.

Everyone was silent now as they walked. The gloom of the forest and the exhaustion they felt left them all with little to say as they kept pushing onwards.

"Ouch," said Madeleine, bumping into Bryn. She rubbed her nose. "What did you stop for?" The woodsman put his finger to his lips and motioned for them to hide swiftly. Alfie and Amy dived behind a couple of large oak trees while Madeleine and Robin disappeared like monkeys into their branches. Alfie crouched behind his tree looking around for Bryn, but he was nowhere to be seen. He had simply melted into the forest. They soon heard footsteps, muffled by the forest floor. Then came men's voices too . . . three different ones. Amy shot Alfie a nervous glance as she hunkered down lower among the tree roots.

"Look, Ulric, I'm telling you – Aggie the thatcher's wife said they came this way," said one of the voices. "Look, you can see they've been walking here."

"I believe you," said a second voice. "Maybe there are strangers out here, but we've walked miles from home, my belly is empty and it's getting late. There's a storm on its way too – my right knee is playing up again."

"Hugh and his magical right knee!" said a third voice, much closer now. "The only reason you know it's going to rain is because there's great bloomin' grey clouds in the sky. We're staying out 'til we find this lot. Aggie said they had sacks with them. Probably thieving or poaching. Turn them in and there'll be a reward for us. Wouldn't mind some of their loot too, if they have been thievin'."

Alfie quietly stood up and peeked through a

fork in the lower branches to catch a glimpse of the men. They had stopped near where the group was hidden. Two of them were tall and stocky, not far off Bryn's height. The other, the one who had spoken last, was shorter and wiry, with shrewd little eyes. Of the three men, Alfie knew he was the one to watch out for.

"We've lost the trail here, Rafe," said Ulric. "Think they heard us coming?"

"Wouldn't be surprised with Hugh here whining about his empty guts."

Alfie dropped silently back behind the tree as Rafe, the man with the shrewd eyes, glanced around. Everything went quiet – the men must have realized they were hidden nearby and Alfie could hear them trying to walk as silently as possible as they searched. He was sure his pounding heart would give him away as Hugh crept towards the tree behind which he was hiding. Alfie silently backed around the trunk as the man came closer. Finding a hollow in the trunk of the tree, he quickly squeezed inside, but he was a second too late. The big man, Ulric, had been creeping around the other side, and he reached in with two great hands and wrenched Alfie from his hiding place.

"Got one!" he shouted.

10

The King's Rangers

Alfie struggled frantically to free himself from the man's grasp.

"That one was mine," shouted Hugh. Alfie's heart sank as he heard a yell from Amy.

"Got another one," said Rafe. "The others must be close by."

Alfie tried to fight against his huge captor, but it was no use. He might as well have fought one of the trees. All he achieved was earning a cuff to the head that made his ears ring as he was dragged to the clearing with Amy. The men searched them and snatched the bag Alfie was

162

carrying slung across his shoulders. He hoped Madeleine and Robin would be sensible enough to stay hidden.

"Should we keep looking for the others?" asked Hugh.

"Plenty of time for that," said Rafe. "Right lads," he said, taking for granted short-haired Amy was a boy. "You're not from round here, are you?" His eyes narrowed as he looked hard at Amy. "Especially this one."

"So what?" said Alfie, trying to make himself look as tall and unafraid as possible. "Since when was being from somewhere else a crime?"

"Since I say it is," Rafe smirked.

"And who are you? The quee— I mean the king of England?" spat Amy.

"Watch your tongue, lad, or I'll have Ulric cut it out for you." Ulric's hand rested on the hilt of a knife at his belt. "As deputy warden I represent the king's interests in these parts. And my rangers here help me round up trespassers and poachers. So, maybe you'd like to tell us what you're up to before we take you to the warden."

"We're just passing through, sir," said Alfie, wondering if he could talk his way out if they both stayed calm.

"Sir?" said Rafe, looking around at the others. They both laughed. "Sir! I likes that. Shows respect. But I'm not buying it. I think we've caught us a gang of thieves here." He pulled Alfie's bag from Ulric's hands. "Let's see what you've got."

Rafe struggled with the leather cord fastening the bag as the other two leaned over to see what was in it. Giving up on the knot, he pulled a knife from his belt and sliced through the cord. A high-pitched trilling noise filled the air as a small silver whirlwind exploded from the bag.

"Sparky!" Alfie called out in astonishment as the little bird zipped about Rafe's head, scratching at him with its tiny silver talons. He couldn't believe that the little idiot had sneaked into his bag *again*. Rafe shrieked and dropped the bag. "Get it off me, get it off me!" he yelled.

Ulric and Hugh stood in stunned silence at the bizarre sight. Alfie and Amy tried to use the disturbance to free themselves from the men, but their grip was too tight.

Ulric finally took action by raising one of his great fists and knocking the bird out of the air, as if swatting a fly.

"No!" cried Alfie as the silver sparrow spiralled to the ground, waddled dizzily for a few steps then fell forwards, a disturbing *sprong* echoing from inside its casing.

"You killed it!" screamed Amy, biting Ulric's arm, which was holding her fast.

"Do that again, and I'll do the same to you," Ulric bellowed, raising his foot to stomp on the little bird.

"Ulric! Leave it!" said Rafe, as though scolding a disobedient dog. He picked up Sparky, its wings flopping uselessly by its sides as he shook the dirt from it. "Solid silver, that. Not in bad nick either. Should get a pretty penny from one of the nobs. So lad, where'd you nick it from? And what else you got?" He tossed the limp bird to Hugh and leaned forwards, his thin face so close that Alfie could smell the stale beer on his breath.

There was a sudden rustle in the trees. Hugh yelped as an arrow whizzed by his ear.

"Let them go," shouted Robin's voice.

Alfie looked up through the trees to spot Robin perched astride a branch, another arrow already nocked to his bow and aimed down at Rafe.

"Better do as he says," yelled Madeleine from the next tree. "There's ten of us up here. All with arrows pointed at your heads."

Ulric and Hugh immediately released Alfie and

Amy and put their hands in the air.

"It's OK, see? We've let them go."

Rafe glared at them. "Idiots," he shouted, lunging for Alfie, who was a second too slow in running for the trees. Alfie cried out as he was dragged back and gripped around the chest with a blade held firmly to his neck. Amy stopped, looking unsure whether to stay or run.

"Run and I take his head off," said Rafe. He nodded up to Madeleine and Robin. "If you were going to shoot you'd have done it already. Aggie told us there are only five of you. You might be all talk, but I'm not. Throw down those weapons and get down from that tree, or I start throwing pieces of your friend to the boar."

Alfie tried to shout out, to tell the twins not to obey, but Rafe's eyes gleamed menacingly as he gripped his throat so tightly he couldn't even cough. There was a soft *thud* as the twins dropped their bows and swung down from the trees. Hugh had already recaptured Amy and the twins were soon held firmly too.

There was a flash of lightning overhead, closely followed by a rumble of thunder as large drops of rain began to patter down through the leaves.

"Got ourselves a couple of poachers too, by the

looks of things!" said Ulric picking up the bows. "Thieves and poachers. Should earn us a nice reward."

"What about the other one?" asked Hugh, scanning the trees.

"Long gone," said Rafe. "Sensible man, your dad," he smirked at Alfie. "Leaving his kids to take the fall, and by fall I mean..." He held his fist above his head as though he was pulling on a rope and let his head flop to the side, tongue hanging out. The foresters laughed as Alfie twisted and struggled.

"Now what's this?" said Rafe, dragging Alfie back. "You bin holding out on us?" Alfie flinched as the knife slipped under the leather strip around his neck, flipping the talisman out on to his tunic. Rafe's eyes gleamed and he whistled softly as he saw the gold.

"Now would you look at that? I think I'll 'ave this little trinket for meself."

"No!" yelled Alfie, fear gripping his heart as the one thing shielding them from the wraith was torn from his neck. "Give it back!"

"Bryn, Bryn!" Madeleine began to scream, echoed by Robin.

"Enough!" yelled Rafe. "Bring them!"

He began to drag Alfie back the way they had

come, Ulric dragging the struggling twins behind him and Hugh following with Amy who had joined in the twins' cry.

"Bryn, BRYN!"

A terrible roar, louder than the thunder overhead, tore through the forest. The ground seemed to tremble below Alfie's feet as something thundered towards them. *A stag, a boar?* Nothing could have prepared Alfie for what he saw crashing through the trees, teeth bared and claws raised.

"BEAR!" screamed the men, dropping their captives. Alfie's jaw hung loose at the sight of the huge beast that reared up in front of them to roar right into the face of Ulric, who stood directly in its path. Alfie somehow gathered his wits enough to grab the talisman from Rafe's hand as the man turned tail and fled.

"Keep still," hissed Robin. Alfie could hardly do anything else; he was frozen to the spot, legs shaking as if they had a mind of their own. The bear swung its head from side to side, looking at them, then let out a gigantic snort, dropped back on to all fours and galloped after the disappearing men.

Alfie dropped to the ground, gasping as he tried to stop shuddering. He crawled over to the others, who seemed to be trying to regain control of their own legs too.

"Will it come back?" panted Amy. "Should we run?"

"It could outrun us," said Robin. "But it seemed to be set on catching those guys."

"I almost felt sorry for them," said Madeleine. "Almost."

"Do you think Bryn's OK?" said Alfie, grabbing a branch and pulling himself up, not trusting his shaky legs. "You don't think the bear. . ."

"I think we'd have heard something if he'd run into it," said Amy. "But where is he? Why did he just leave us like that?"

Her words pricked at the back of Alfie's mind. Why hadn't Bryn come to help them? Had something happened to him? He liked Bryn a great deal; he didn't even want to consider the fact that the woodsman had just left them.

"Bryn! Bryn, come out!" Alfie hissed, not daring to shout any louder. There was no answer. He sighed and tied the talisman back around his neck, relieved that he had managed to get it back. Without the talisman shielding the magic inside him, the wraith might have easily found them.

"Look," said Madeleine, picking up the silver

sparrow from the forest floor. It fluttered weakly in her hands as she held it out towards Alfie.

"Sparky!" said Alfie. "You poor thing!" He took the bird carefully from Madeleine and turned it over in his hands. It was making little clicking and whirring noises. He shook it very gently, its head flopped from side to side and he heard something rattling inside.

"I think a spring came loose," said Robin. "I have my mini screwdrivers back at the castle – I could take a look at it. But first, we should get back up into the trees while we wait for Bryn." He looked around quickly. "We should probably do that now!"

Alfie gently stroked the bird's head with his finger then wrapped it in a piece of cloth, placing it carefully in his bag before clambering up into one of the oaks with the others. They perched on a branch each, hidden by leaves as they watched and waited. *Where was he?* Alfie wondered.

"Shh!" said Amy suddenly. There was a distant rustling. Someone was coming. Alfie strained to see through the gloom. Was it Bryn, or were the men returning? Or even worse, the bear. A low whistle rang through the trees. Alfie heaved a sigh of relief.

"Bryn!" he cried, dropping down from the

branch to meet the dishevelled woodsman.

"Are you all OK?" asked Bryn, clapping his hand on Alfie's back and hurrying over to check on the others.

"We're fine," said Robin. "Apart from Spar—" He caught Alfie's eye and steered away from mentioning the silver bird. "But what happened to you?"

"I couldn't get back to you." He looked down at his feet. "The bear, I—"

"You ran into the bear?" exclaimed Madeleine. "No wonder you didn't come to help us. You're lucky it didn't attack you. You should have seen it go for those men. They were awful, but I hope it didn't catch them."

"It didn't," said Bryn. "I followed until it stopped chasing them. But they won't be back tonight."

"I'm not surprised," said Amy. "That thing was terrifying. I hope it doesn't come back for us."

"Come on," said Bryn. "We've covered enough distance; we should be safe. It's getting late and we need to rest if we're to keep on going. Let's find somewhere to eat and sleep."

11

The Heart of the Night

Alfie sighed with relief as he lay back on sweet-smelling bouncy hay and wolfed down his share of the bread and cheese Bryn had passed around. They were eating their meal in a barn which Bryn had talked a farmer into letting them use for the night with the last few coins in his pocket.

"We're nearly out of food," said Bryn, looking sadly at the last loaf and hunk of cheese in the sack. "I've paid the farmer for some breakfast, but that's all the money gone. We'll have to forage for anything else we need, and that's going to slow us down."

"We could just buy some food in the next village," said Amy, peeling a boiled egg.

"With what?" asked Robin. "Me and Maddie have some money that Mum gave us, but it's not like we can spend it here."

"I was thinking we could use this." Amy pulled a little leather pouch from her belt and tossed it to Bryn. Alfie heard a loud *chink* as Bryn caught it and tipped out a handful of silver coins.

"Whoa. Where did you get that!" said Alfie, staring at her, wide-eyed.

"The weasely guy that caught you dropped it." Amy shrugged. "It would have been rude *not* to take it."

"Do you think there might be enough here to hire a horse and cart, like the one Barnabas had?" asked Alfie.

Bryn was staring at the little pile of coins. "Maybe. The farmer seems a decent bloke. I'll ask if I can borrow one of his in the morning. We'd still need to figure out where to get a boat to take us out to the island, but with a bit of luck we'll be back here late tomorrow."

"That means we should be able to get home by the following night," said Alfie. He chewed his lip. That meant they'd get back to Orin and Ashford three days from when the wraith attacked them. "Do you think they'll be OK? Will the witch really be able to help them, and those people in the village?"

"If anyone can, it's her," said Bryn. "Now, let's get some shut-eye."

They each found a cosy spot to sleep in the hay. Alfie snuggled into a little nest in the straw and pulled his cloak over himself as Bryn extinguished one of the oil lamps the farmer had lent them. He lay awake for a while, grateful for the soft glow of the lamp as he listened to the distant hoots of the owls in the nearby forest, and the gentle flatulence of the cow that shared the barn with them. Robin had worked out that they had travelled over thirty miles by foot and cart but they were still only halfway there and the muscles in Alfie's legs were already starting to stiffen and ache. Was that enough distance? Bryn seemed to think they were safe enough, but had they really left the wraith behind? And Agrodonn – was he out there looking for them too?

He pounded the straw into a more comfortable pillow and pulled the cloak up to his chin, his hand automatically clutching the talisman around his neck. He had been very lucky not to lose it to the men who had ambushed them. Orin had told him that it kept the magic inside him subdued and hidden. It was more important than ever that it stay that way with the wraith searching for it. It took him longer than the others to fall asleep, chilled by the thought of being pursued by a creature that could drain the very life from its victims.

The wraith moved swiftly north, strengthened by the life force of the Great Druid. It had felt the magic in the castle – it had been there at one time, but not now. It had drifted aimlessly, briefly catching a hint of the magic's vibration, but had been unable to latch on to it, as though it was hidden. But then, for a brief moment, it was as though a curtain had lifted. The magic had shone out like a beacon, and the wraith was heeding its call. Over fields, over heather, through forests that fell silent in its wake, it was coming.

By two large oak trees it stopped. This was where the magic had revealed itself; the air still hummed from its energy. It was no longer here, hidden once more, but the wraith could feel it now. It could see the trails it had left as it had moved on from this place. The wraith followed.

Alfie scrambled from his straw bed, heart hammering as Amy's screams tore through the still night air.

"What? What is it!" he yelled, spinning around as he searched for the cause of her panic. Bryn was already on his feet, wooden staff gripped between both hands, ready to fight.

"It's found us," cried Amy, her face bloodless in the light of the oil lamp. "The thing, the wraith, it's coming, now!"

The twins were scrabbling through their sacks for their bows and arrows.

Alfie didn't stop to ask if she was certain – her face said it clearly enough.

"What do we do?" he asked Bryn. The woodsman raised the bar that secured the great door, pushed it open and stared out into the night.

"What are you doing? You'll let it in!" cried Madeleine.

"The door won't stop it," said Amy, grabbing the lamp and trying to relight the other with shaking hands. "Help me light this! It only travels by night, maybe light can hold it back."

Madeleine and Robin rushed to help Amy. Alfie tried to keep his legs from trembling as he stood by Bryn, searching the blackness. "What does it look like?" he asked. But then he saw it. It was as though the black heart of the night itself was heading towards them. He scrambled away from the door as it swept towards the barn. Madeleine and Robin had drawn their bows and stood with arrows aimed towards the door, knuckles white. Amy stood at Alfie's side, holding the lanterns out in front of her like talismans of her own.

"Stay back!" roared Bryn, backing up as the wraith floated through the door. He lashed out with the staff but it went straight through the shadowy creature. He dropped to his knees with a cry as the creature flowed straight through him.

"Bryn, are you OK?" cried Alfie.

"The voices," gasped Bryn. "Such pain and sadness."

The wraith hovered in the centre of the barn in its cloaked human form. Little black tendrils floated around its edges, like black ink swirling through water. A noise was coming from it, a soft hissing. No – voices. They whispered just at the edges of Alfie's hearing, then suddenly they were all speaking the same words.

Him. Him. He hasss it. It raised an arm towards Alfie.

Thud!

Thud!

Two arrows travelled through the wraith and into the barn wall. For a brief second Alfie saw two holes in the creature. They closed almost instantly as it began to drift slowly towards them.

Take it. Mussst take it.

They all backed up as it drifted closer. The lanterns Amy held out seemed to be keeping it back to a certain extent, but a long tendril finger was stretching out towards Alfie. Was it just going to take the magic, or was it going to drain the life from them as it did to Orin? Maybe both. Alfie looked around the barn frantically. How could he fight something that was like smoke? Amy held the lamps higher and the wraith recoiled slightly. It was like a moth, drawn to the magic and the warmth, then flinching at its touch. Suddenly Alfie knew what to do.

Snatching one of the lamps from Amy he hurled it to the straw-strewn floor below the wraith. It smashed, the oil that spilled out immediately catching alight. The wraith's souls shrieked as it whirled into the darkest corner of the barn.

"What are you doing?" shouted Amy as the flames roared higher, fed by the dry straw. "You'll burn us all alive!"

"I won't," said Alfie. He began to breathe deeply, just as Orin had taught him, calming his beating heart as he held out his hand towards the flames.

Go on, then, he whispered, reaching down to the magic deep inside him and prodding it awake. *Do what you do. Feed.* As the magic welled up inside him, Alfie stretched out his fingers. *It's just like the candle in Orin's study*, he told himself just as he concentrated on the flames and slowly began to draw the energy from the roaring fire. The flames stopped licking their way across the floor and began to flow towards Alfie's hand, fading out as they touched his palm and he drew their energy into himself.

"The fire's going out!" cried Madeleine.

"What's happening to Bryn?" gasped Robin. Alfie barely heard his cousin's words as he focussed on drawing the power of the fire into himself. The wraith was creeping forwards as the fire died down. The last of the flames flickered out, leaving the barn in darkness, save for the sputtering lamp in Amy's hands.

There was a shout from Bryn, almost a growl, as the wraith shot past him towards Alfie. The twins and Amy scattered but Alfie held fast, the talisman on his chest glowing bright white. Just before the wraith hurtled into him Alfie threw his arms wide, drew on the magic and focussed. A bright orb of light formed in each of his hands. The wraith stopped in its tracks as the light illuminated the entire barn. A low keening noise came from it as it stretched its hands towards Alfie despite the pain the light seemed to be causing it. Alfie focussed and a wind began to build up around him. He concentrated it in front of himself, Amy and the twins – driving back the wraith as it fought against the wind and light, trying to reach him.

"Keep it up, Al," shouted Amy as Alfie began to walk forwards, pushing the wraith back out into the night which was starting to turn into dawn. Bryn had clambered to his feet as Alfie drove the wraith past him. There seemed to be something wrong with his face and shoulders but Alfie couldn't look, he had to keep concentrating.

As he drove the wraith outside and prepared to blast it away with a huge gust of wind, a deep growl behind him made him turn and falter. It was Bryn – something was happening to him. Hair sprouted from his skin and his huge shoulders tore his shirt apart as claws sprang from his fingers. The orbs in Alfie's hands faded as he stared in horror at a creature he had seen only hours ago. A giant bear.

"Alfie, the wraith!" cried Robin. Alfie staggered and tried to pull himself together in the face of two threats. The wraith had gathered itself and was inching forwards again. With every scrap of might Alfie summoned up another blinding orb and hurled it straight into the wraith, sending it screaming away into the near dawn. With a mighty roar the bear took off after it, disappearing into the forest. Alfie fell to the floor panting as the others collapsed around him.

"The bear..." said Amy at last. "The one that saved us from the foresters – it was ... *Bryn?*"

"He's a shapeshifter, like Caspian," said Robin, eyes wide, as if he didn't believe the words coming out of his own mouth. "Why didn't he tell us?"

"Maybe he thought we'd be afraid of him?" said Madeleine.

Alfie found himself unable to answer as he tried to process what had happened. Bryn had turned into a bear in the forest and chased away the men that were threatening them. *That* was why he hadn't come to help them, because he *had* helped them. What if the bear came back to the barn? Surely it couldn't be dangerous – it was Bryn! But his eyes and that roar had been so ferocious. Alfie didn't know what to think.

"Do you think it will come back?" asked Madeleine.

"The wraith?" asked Alfie, sitting up. "Maybe not tonight. It's nearly light outside and I don't think it travels by day. You saw how it hated the light. We're safe today at least."

"What about Bryn?" asked Amy. They stared out into the forest.

"Maybe we should go and look for him?" said Alfie, though he didn't trust his legs to even carry him out of the barn.

"When it gets lighter," said Robin. "We don't want to run into the wraith."

Alfie sat on a bale of hay, hugging his knees tight to his chest as Robin and Madeleine swept dirt and straw over the scene of the fire.

"That thing you did with the light and the wind?" asked Amy, sitting down next to him. "Did Orin teach you to do that?"

"Kind of," said Alfie. "He showed me how to feed the magic on energy and create things with it."

"Was it hard?"

"I didn't really think about it," said Alfie. "It was like . . . instinct."

"Well it certainly makes me feel safer, knowing you can do that." Amy smiled. "I think you're going to be a pretty awesome druid."

"I doubt it. I can't get my head round the stuff

in any of those books Orin wanted me to read, but Robin finds it easy. Madeleine is way better than I'll ever be with herbs and wounds and stuff."

"But you've got magic!" said Madeleine. "That's more than any of us!"

"Magic that was just given to me, and I can't do much with. Magic that keeps putting everyone I care about in danger." He thought back to the hare. "Magic that tries to make me do things I don't want to do. Orin wanted to teach me much more than mastering the magic inside me. He wanted me to carry on his knowledge to help our world, but I don't think I'm cut out for it. It's just too much."

As the early dawn light crept over the fields, they ventured out of the barn. It was easy to track Bryn's bear prints in the moist forest floor as they hurried through the forest.

"The prints are pretty far apart," said Madeleine. "He was running really fast."

"Let's just hope it wasn't fast enough to catch up with that thing," said Alfie, pushing ahead.

After following the trail for a few minutes, Alfie stopped dead. The trees around them were covered in deep scratches. Had Bryn actually tried to fight the wraith? Maybe in his bear form he didn't realize what a terrible idea that was. He bit his lip.

"Oh no," said Amy quietly. "Alfie, look." Among the ferns lay a large muddy body dressed only in torn trousers. Bryn. Alfie forced his reluctant legs to walk towards him.

"Give me a hand," he said to the others as he struggled to roll the huge man over.

"He doesn't seem to have any injuries," said Madeleine as they all strained to heave him over. As Bryn finally flopped on to his back, Amy fell back and scrambled away from him.

"Oh no, oh no," she whispered.

Alfie's breath caught in his throat as he stared at Bryn's face and took in the symbol traced on his forehead. A black cross.

"Bryn," said Robin, nervously patting the man's face. "Bryn, can you hear me?"

Madeleine checked his breathing and pulse and sighed. "He's just like the others – there's no way he's walking out of these woods on his own." She looked up at Alfie. "We should get him back to the barn. Any ideas?"

Alfie looked around. "If we can find some branches we could make a kind of stretcher using one of our cloaks. Robin, help me look."

"Are you kidding, Al?" she asked. "Can't you just

make one, like you did with those balls of light?"

"I don't know," mumbled Alfie. "Maybe, but I haven't done anything like that before. I'd need to feed it again."

Madeleine seemed to sense his fear of using the magic a second time.

"It's OK," she said gently. "I saw a wheelbarrow back in the barn. I'll go get it."

Alfie smiled gratefully as she sprinted back to the barn. He sank into an awkward silence with Amy and Robin as they sat watching Bryn's still body. Orin, Ashford, and now Bryn. They were on their own now. Would the witch really be able to help?

"Got it!" shouted Madeleine at last, as she came crashing through the forest with the barrow.

Each taking a limb, they hoisted Bryn's heavy body on to the barrow and began to carefully wheel him back to the barn. They had to keep taking turns, two at a time. Alfie couldn't have imagined just how heavy the great man would be. The sun was already climbing high as they finally reached the barn, dragged Bryn inside and pulled him on to a large bed of straw.

"What now?" asked Robin.

Alfie's mind was whirring. What *could* they do?

"Well, Bryn's plan is ruined," he sighed. "Even if the farmer will lend us a horse and cart, we don't know the way without Bryn, and I'm not even sure I remember how to get back to the castle." He put his hand into his pocket and touched the vial of black liquid that the raven had brought them. He wished they had taken Muninn's advice and just gone home. Surely the future couldn't have been any worse than it was likely to be now? Maybe it wasn't too late, if they could leave Bryn somewhere safe. But was anywhere safe with the wraith around?

"I know the way," said Robin.

Alfie stared at his cousin.

"No you don't," scoffed Madeleine. "You might remember the roads and signposts from when we went up on the school bus, but none of those exist here! There's no way you could get us there, Robin."

"Oh really?" said Robin. He pulled a sheet of thick parchment from his sack and unfolded it. "This was in one of Orin's books that I brought back from Alfie's library. It's a map of this whole area, dated around twenty years from now. Orin must have drawn it himself after flights on Artan." He pointed to a little cluster of islands on the map.

"That's where we're going, and here's where we are now." He pulled a compass from his pocket and placed it on the map. "We need to keep going in that direction, following these roads and tracks," he said, lightly tracing a route north-east with a pencil. When he was satisfied with the route he had drawn to a harbour nearest to the islands, he sat back on his heels and looked up at Alfie. "Now all we need is the transport!"

Alfie gave his cousin a grateful little punch on the arm. Even though they weren't sure if they could find a way out to the island, at least they knew where it was. It was a start.

"Before we do anything, are we going to discuss the fact that Bryn can turn into a bear?" asked Madeleine.

"Heads up," interrupted Amy from the door. "Visitors!"

Robin folded the map and put it back in his pocket. Alfie quickly swept Bryn's hair forward to cover the cross on his forehead and pulled his cloak over him so that it looked as though he was sleeping, just as the farmer and his wife appeared at the door with a loaf of bread, some ham and a pitcher of milk.

"Breakfast," said the farmer. Alfie gladly took

the food.

"Thank you. And thanks for letting us stay here last night." He glanced at the others and Robin gave him a meaningful nod. "We saw you have horses. Well, we were wondering if we could borrow a couple, and maybe a cart. Just until tomorrow. We can pay you," he added quickly, jingling the bag of coins Amy had acquired. The farmer took it, counted out the coins and had a quiet conversation with his wife.

"I'm sorry," he said at last. "There's not enough here for us to take the risk. We don't know you. If you don't come back how are we going to afford to replace the horses?"

"What if two of us stayed here and helped on the farm?" said Robin. "You could keep an eye on us that way, and even lock us up in here at night so we can't run off. That way you can be sure you'd get your horses back."

The farmer rubbed his chin as he weighed up the offer.

"We could use some help today, and the money won't go amiss," said his wife, giving him a sharp nudge. "Especially with the tax collectors due any day now."

Alfie could see the farmer was on the verge of

agreeing, but then his eyes narrowed as they fell on Bryn lying motionless under his cloak. "What's wrong with him?" he asked sharply. "Why is he still sleeping?"

"He's fine!" said Alfie quickly. "It's just ... just..."

"A fever," said Robin quickly. "He had bad toothache and it brought on a fever. That's why we need to borrow the horses – he wanted us to fetch someone he trusts to treat him."

The farmer circled around to try to get a look at Bryn, Alfie noticed that he was avoiding getting too close and was grateful – he didn't want him to spot the cross on his forehead. Taking a long wooden rake leaning against the wall the man prodded Bryn with the wooden end. He didn't move.

"He's sleeping," said Madeleine, her hands clenched tightly in front of her. "I gave him some medicine to help with the pain. You won't be able to wake him."

The farmer prodded Bryn again, this time so hard that he rolled slightly. Alfie crossed his fingers as Bryn's hair parted slightly to reveal a little of the black mark on his forehead, but the farmer saw it.

"A black spot!" said the farmer, dropping the

rake. "You brought plague on to *my* farm?"

"No, no it isn't plague," said Amy, brushing aside Bryn's hair to reveal the cross. "Look, it's just a mark"

"Out," said the farmer, covering his nose and mouth with his sleeve as he held his hand out in front of him to stop them approaching. "Take him and get out."

"But what about the horses?" asked Alfie, his heart dropping into his boots. "Please! We need them. You've got to lend them to us!"

"OUT! And take your disease with you," roared the farmer as he practically ran from the barn.

There was a stunned silence as their hopes of finding the witch were dashed, again. Alfie looked down at Bryn. How were they supposed to move him? Where could they take him?

The farmer's wife remained, her sleeve held up to her nose. "Is it true?" she asked. "Is it ..." her voice fell to a whisper, "the Black Death?"

"No. I swear it," said Alfie, beseechingly. "I'm sorry we lied about the toothache. He is ill, really ill, but it's nothing you can catch. We've been with him for days and we're fine. Look..." He stripped off his own tunic and span around so that she could see he was clear of marks and had no lumps around his neck or beneath his arms. "We just need the horses to get this person who can help him." Alfie didn't think it wise to tell her that they were trying to find a witch. "Please, can you lend them to us? Or let us stay here until we find another way to travel?"

She looked Alfie long and hard in the eyes. "I believe you," she said at last. She sighed and sat down on a little wooden stool. "But I can't lend you our horses. He's not a heartless man, my husband. He lost his mother and brothers to the Black Death when he was a boy. He still has the night terrors. He wakes screaming and checks the whole family to see if we've taken ill." She looked around at them. "So you can understand his fears?"

They all nodded.

"He won't be back until midday. The most I can do is to let you stay a few hours. There may be someone who could sell you a donkey in town, and perhaps you could pay the doctor to come up and take a look at him. But you must be gone by noon."

Alfie thanked her profusely as she left, then sank down on to the straw with the others, head in his hands. They had to keep on moving. What were they going to do now?

12

The Tournament

Alfie figured it was about nine o'clock as he hurried towards the nearest town with Madeleine, hoping against hope they'd find someone to sell or lend them a horse. Robin and Amy had stayed behind in the barn with Bryn in case the farmer returned. They planned to make a shelter in the forest where Amy and Madeleine would stay guarding the woodsman while Alfie would travel on to Demon Rock with Robin to direct him. He didn't have a clue how the witch would travel back with them, or how they would get Bryn back to Hexbridge Castle, but Amy had convinced him to only worry about one thing at a time. At least Amy and Madeleine would be safe; the wraith was only after him. He couldn't help wishing they had brought Artan despite Caspian's warning. The bear could have flown them all the way to the island itself and back within a day.

"There's a storm coming," said Madeleine.

Alfie looked up. The sun was fairly bright but distant clouds on the horizon were closing in.

They passed many other people travelling into the town as they hurried along, following the directions the farmer's wife had given them.

"There must be something happening today," said Madeleine, as several fancy coaches trundled past.

The procession got thicker as it met other groups streaming towards the entrance gate of a huge castle. Alfie was tempted to follow to see where they were going, but headed instead into the town square. He stared around in surprise. The whole town was deserted but for a small boy throwing a stick for a scruffy mongrel. They went from shop to shop, staring in through the windows, but all of them were closed.

"They've all gone to the tournament," called the boy, wrestling the stick from the dog's jaws, then throwing it far across the market square. Alfie and

Madeleine wandered over to join him. He was a couple of years younger than them and dressed quite shabbily, even compared to the slept-in clothes Alfie was wearing.

"I'm ... Alfred, and this is my cousin, Maud," said Alfie, sitting down next to him.

"I'm Henry, like the king," grinned the boy. "'Cept I don't 'ave his bags of gold to sleep on. This is Stinker." Alfie tried not to screw up his nose as the dog raced up to them and dropped the stick, panting proudly. He could see where it got its name. Stinker looked and smelled as though he had been rolling around in cowpats.

"Nice to meet you, Henry," said Alfie, shaking the boy's dirty hand. "Maybe you can help us? We need a horse. Is there anyone around here who could lend us one?"

"No one's going to lend a horse to strangers," said Henry. "But I know someone who would mebbe sell you one. He drives a hard bargain though. How much you got?"

Alfie poured out the silver coins from his pouch into his tunic. The boy let out a low whistle as he looked longingly at the money.

"It's more than I've ever set me eyes on," said Henry. "But I'm not sure it's enough for a horse."

"Could you take us to this man and help us bargain for one of his horses?" asked Madeleine.

Henry scratched his grubby cheek. "I could, but he's at the tournament and it's two shillings each to get in."

"We'll pay," said Alfie, scooping the coins back into the pouch.

"Nah," said Henry. "You'll need every penny you've got. I've a better idea. Come on, I'll get us all in for free. You stay here, Stinker," Henry said firmly as the dog began to follow. "Now don't look at me like that, you know it don't work on me. I'll be back soon."

Stinker watched mournfully as they hurried away to join the crowd.

"We're in luck!" said Henry, spotting a cart full of barrels that had stopped where the road began to slope up towards the castle. The driver was feeding the donkey from a nosebag, but it seemed to be refusing to go any further.

"All those barrels are too heavy for it," called Henry as he hurried over to the man. "How about we take a couple and roll them up to the castle for you, uncle?"

"Well, we won't be going anywhere otherwise," said the man. "But how do I know you won't run off with them? What's in it for you?"

"We'll walk ahead of you so you can keep an eye on us. We just want to get into the tournament and we don't have any money – all you have to do is tell the guards we're working for you bringing refreshments. It won't even be a lie. What do you say?"

"Nice going," said Alfie as he put his shoulder to one of the heavy barrels and began to roll it towards the castle. Henry and Madeleine were rolling another just behind him, followed by the donkey, which seemed much happier to be pulling a lighter cart.

The guards were taking money from some of the people passing through the gates, and waving through most of the fancy coaches and the carts carrying supplies. Alfie thought they'd be able to slip straight inside, but one of the guards blocked their way.

"What's in the barrels?" he demanded.

"Er. . ." Alfie stammered, as he realized he didn't know.

"They're with me," called the man driving the cart. "We're carrying mead." He hopped down from the cart, removed a large cork stopper from Alfie's barrel and poured out a cupful. The guard sniffed it then downed the whole cup in one go.

"Not bad," he said, wiping his mouth with the back of his hand and waving them through. "Don't set up too far away. I'll come by for more later."

"Be nice if he was even considering paying," grumbled the mead seller as they passed through the gates.

The castle grounds were huge. Much bigger than those of Hexbridge Castle. They helped the mead seller set up and thanked him for getting them inside, before leaving to explore the grounds. The crowd was gathering in a huge field, the centre of which had been ringed off. At one end was a large wooden stand which, judging by their clothes, seated high-ranking nobles. At the other end were ringed targets, similar to the ones the twins used for archery practice. Two well-dressed men had stepped up to their marks to the cheers of the crowd, and were taking it in turns to fire at the targets.

"It's an archery tournament!" cried Madeleine.

"This morning it is," said Henry. "I'm not so bothered about archery," he sniffed. "I was going to sneak in for the jousting this afternoon, now *that's* exciting."

"Can't we stay and watch, Alfie?" asked Madeleine, ignoring Henry's slight against her sport.

"What do you think, Maddie?" asked Alfie, one eyebrow raised.

"OK, OK, I know. No time," said Madeleine, looking ruefully over her shoulder at the archers as Henry led them towards the tents of the merchants and blacksmiths. They stopped at a couple of food stalls to stock up on bread, a whole roast chicken and some apples. Alfie noticed Henry gazing hungrily at the food and bought him a bowl of salt pork and beans from a man stirring a large pot. Henry wolfed it down greedily, popping a few chunks of the meat into his pocket.

"For Stinker," he grinned, wiping his greasy fingers on his trousers as he handed the bowl back.

Alfie couldn't help but warm towards the boy who, hungry as he was, saved some of his meal for the scruffy little dog.

"There's Barrett," said Henry, pointing towards a fat man who was sitting in the shade of a tent eating a chicken leg as a small boy hurried around pouring water and oats for the horses tethered at either side of the tent.

"I don't like the look of him," muttered Madeleine as Henry led them towards the tent. Alfie agreed. Barrett had shrewd little piggy eyes and an ugly sneer.

"What do you want?" he barked at Henry as the boy stopped in front of the tent. "Get out of here, before your stink drives the customers away. I've just sold those two horses to Lord Lumley and his aide will be here to pick them up any minute now."

"We are customers," said Henry, puffing out his chest. "My friends Alfred and Maud would like to buy one of your finest horses."

Barrett almost choked on his mouthful of chicken as he burst out laughing. "You? Customers?" he roared, flinging the chicken bones aside. "Get out of here before I have you thrown out. I'm guessing none of you paid to get in."

Henry ducked as Barrett aimed a cuff at his head. "We are customers," he shouted, grabbing the pouch from Alfie and jangling it in front of him.

Barrett's piggy eyes lit up as he sucked the grease from his fingers. He took the pouch and sifted through it, his lips moving slightly as he swiftly added up the coins. Henry snatched it back from him the second he finished. "We'll give it to you for that horse." He pointed out the largest and finest of the horses tethered nearby.

"That one?" laughed Barrett, shaking his head. "Well, you've a sense of humour, if nothing else."

"OK, so not that one," snapped Alfie. "But we

need a horse and you've seen that we can pay you right now. What can you sell us?"

The man stopped laughing and got to his feet. "Well, there is one steed that I'd let go for that price, at a pinch. Come with me."

Alfie sighed with relief as they followed Barrett past several tents to an area where several more horses were grazing. They all looked fit and healthy, and quite capable of carrying two boys the rest of the distance to the coast by Demon Rock.

"Which one can we buy?" asked Alfie.

Barrett gave a toothy grin as he pointed. "The one behind that brown mare."

Alfie's face fell as he saw the animal Barrett was pointing to – a very old, bandy-legged donkey that was grazing happily alongside the horses.

"You're kidding?" said Henry. "It'd take a week for that one to carry me home, and I only live on the other side of the village!"

"Take it or leave it," laughed Barrett. "No skin off my nose!"

"Sorry," said Henry as they watched Barrett stroll back to his tent, belly jiggling as he laughed to himself. "He's always like that, but I thought it might be worth a try."

"It's OK," sighed Alfie. "We'd better head back to Robin and Amy and figure out what to do next."

"Alfie," said Madeleine. "I know it's not something we'd *ever* usually consider, but, well, what if we took those two horses from the farm? I don't mean steal them. We'd leave the money, and bring them back when we're done."

Alfie stared at her, wide-eyed. He could hardly believe she was suggesting it, but as he fought for an answer his brain began to process the suggestion. He didn't like to even think of taking the horses without permission, but hadn't the farmer almost agreed to lend them out just before he saw the mark on Bryn's forehead? Perhaps it was the only answer, the only way they could get help for Orin, Ashford, and now Bryn too.

"Hey, d'you hear that?" said Henry suddenly, ducking into a roped-off area. "Come on," he beckoned.

Alfie checked that no one was looking before they slipped after Henry. The tents in this area were much fancier than the others. Each had an ornate family crest prominently displayed outside.

"This way," said Henry. He led them straight to a large blue tent by which stood an ornate coach. "Hear that?" Henry asked as they stopped outside.

Someone inside was crying, long shuddering sobs. "Let's see what's up," said Henry, diving through the curtained entrance before Alfie could stop him. Henry seemed to go wherever he pleased without any thought for the consequences, but then so did Madeleine. She was already inside the tent before Alfie could stop her. He shook his head and followed them through.

On a bed of silks and embroidered cushions lay a boy of about fourteen with wavy, chin-length blonde hair. His face was streaked with tears and his left arm was strapped up in a sling. A fine bow and quiver of arrows lay scattered across the floor, as though they had been thrown there.

"Who are you?" he demanded, wiping away his tears as he glared at them. "How dare you come in here!"

"We heard you crying," said Henry, sitting on the end of the bed. "Just wondered what was up, that's all."

"I wasn't crying," lied the boy. "And GET OFF MY BED!"

Alfie had to stifle a laugh at Henry's brazen cheek. "I'm sorry, we'll be on our way," he said, grabbing Henry's arm and pulling him off the bed. He was about to hurry from the tent before the boy called for any guards he might have, but Madeleine had other ideas.

"This is nice," she said, picking up the bow from the floor and stroking it. "Really fine craftsmanship." She raised it and drew back the string, nodded approvingly and placed it on the end of the bed. "Are you any good with it?"

"Any good?" spluttered the boy. "Better than anyone else in my age category. I was going to win this thing, until that swine Percy *accidentally* spooked my horse while I was out riding this morning. Now I can't hold my bow and he's going to win." He sniffed and angrily wiped away the large tear that was rolling off his chin.

"So he made sure you couldn't compete," said Madeleine, shaking her head. "No wonder you're angry. He must have thought he'd have no chance against you."

"He's never come close to beating me," said the boy, sitting up proudly at Madeleine's praise. "If only I could compete. I'd teach him a lesson!"

"Do you mind if I take a look at your arm?" she asked. "Maybe I can do something for it."

"Maud's a healer," said Alfie, as the boy gave her a doubtful look. "A really good one."

The boy winced as Madeleine undid his sling

and examined his arm. "It's not broken," she said at last. "But it's badly bruised and you've pulled the muscles when you fell. I've got some ointment that will help with the pain and healing, but you're not going to be able to hold a bow for a while."

The boy managed to fight back his tears this time, wincing as Madeleine rubbed the ointment on to his arm and strapped the sling back on.

"Thank you. That does feel a little better," he sighed. "I'm Edgar. Edgar Lumley."

"Pleased to meet you," said Alfie. "I'm Alfred, and this is our friend Henry."

"You know, you two look quite alike," said Henry, taking the pot of ointment and giving it a sniff.

Alfie looked from Madeleine to Edgar and was surprised to see that Henry was right. They were about the same height, both had blue eyes and dark blonde hair, although Edgar's was much tidier. They even had similar noses. From a distance it might be hard to tell them apart. As he looked from one to the other, a plan began to form in his head.

"Edgar, can you imagine just how shocked Percy would be if you went out there to compete today?"

"Don't tease me," scowled Edgar. "I'd love to see the look on his little rat face, but it's not going to happen, is it? No matter how good a healer Maud is."

"What if I knew a way Percy would *think* that you were competing against him?" said Alfie, picking one of the arrows from the floor and smoothing its feathers.

"Go on," said Edgar leaning forwards.

"Well, maybe we could make that happen, and all it would cost you is a favour."

Thirty minutes later Alfie stood nervously behind the nobles' stand with Edgar, a cloaked and hooded Madeleine, and a very excited Henry.

"Are you sure you want to do this, Maddie?" Alfie asked, peering around the stand as the crowd cheered for a boy who had just hit the centre of his target.

"Absolutely," she whispered.

Alfie gave her a thumbs-up as he crossed the fingers of his other hand. If his idea was to work, Madeleine had to convince the crowd that she was Edgar. He had agreed to lend them his coach and driver just for competing, but would he stick to his promise if Madeleine lost too badly?

"Right then, I'd better flash my face around,"

Edgar grinned. He removed his sling but arranged his cloak to cover the fact that he was holding the arm stiffly, then strode over to where a smug-looking boy was checking his arrows. Alfie edged closer and strained his ears to hear what they were saying.

"Percy," nodded Edgar as he passed the boy, bow in hand.

"Ed... Edgar," stammered Percy. "I thought ... well I thought you..."

"Weren't competing?" said Edgar, eyebrows raised. "Why ever would you think that? Well, we're up next, I'd better get ready. Looking forward to facing you in the finals." Edgar winked at Alfie as he headed back behind the stand and handed his bow to Madeleine. She threw off her cloak and strapped on Edgar's quiver. She was dressed in a very similar outfit to Edgar.

"How do I look?" she asked.

"Like a born noble," said Edgar, approvingly.

"OK, now for the final touch," said Alfie, looking ruefully at Madeleine's hair. "Henry, did you find some scissors?"

"Just don't ask where I got them," grinned the boy, pulling an ornate pair of silver scissors from his pocket.

Alfie took hold of a lock of Madeleine's hair and raised the scissors. He could almost hear his Aunt Grace shouting at him for even daring to think of what he was about to do.

"Come on, Alfie, we don't have all day!" scolded Madeleine. "If you're not going to chop it off, I will."

A fanfare started up and the crowd cheered loudly.

"Better get moving," said Edgar as a name was called and the crowd cheered again. "That's the first of the finalists. I'm up third."

Alfie swallowed hard and began to chop. Blonde hair rained to the ground as he circled Madeleine, snipping off lock after lock of her wavy hair at chin level.

There was a thud and the crowd murmured – the archer had taken his first shot.

"Not bad," said Henry as he peered around the stand, watching the contest. "Not bad at all."

"How do I look?" asked Madeleine.

Alfie looked from Edgar to Madeleine. "Quite convincing, but it's not going to fool anyone up close."

"She'll be fine if she wears my chaperon," said Edgar, placing a hat on Madeleine's head. It was like a cross between a turban and a hood, with a long strip of fabric that hung down one side and hid part of Madeleine's face. Alfie had seen other people around with similar headwear.

"I think we might get away with this," Alfie smiled.

"As long as you really can shoot," said Edgar, handing Madeleine his bow. "You don't have to win, but try not to embarrass me too much."

"I'll try," said Madeleine in clipped tones as she took the bow.

There was another thud and applause broke out.

"That was a good one," called Henry. "Come and watch his last shot."

Edgar put on the cape Madeleine had been wearing. He put up the hood as they stepped out from behind the stands. Alfie noticed Madeleine was keeping the side of her face that was hidden behind the chaperon turned towards Percy, who kept glancing over. Alfie hoped the boy wasn't getting suspicious.

The archer, a boy of around fifteen, was aiming to take his last shot. About twenty-five paces away was a round white target with a black circle, a little larger than a tennis ball, in the centre. One of the archer's arrows was in the white area just outside of the black circle.

"That one's a miss," said Edgar. "The one inside the black circle is a hit, but it's quite close to the edge, so it's not brilliant. OK, let's watch his next shot."

The crowd was silent as the boy released his arrow. It whistled through the air to thud into the board, hitting the target right on the line between black and white.

"It's touching the black, so it counts as a hit, not a great one though," said Edgar. A weak applause broke out as the archer left the field. "Percy should easily beat that. Watch, here he comes."

Alfie noticed Madeleine taking note of Percy's stance as he stood on his mark and made a great show of selecting an arrow from his quiver.

"Phtt, he's thinking too much about how he looks," she scoffed. Drawing back his bow, Percy released an arrow to thud easily into the black circle.

Alfie's fingernails bit into his palms. "He might be a poser, but he's still a great shot."

Percy's next arrow was a little further out, but the third hit very close to the wooden peg that marked the centre of the target. The crowd cheered loudly as Percy bowed in every direction, then held his bow aloft as though he had already won. He smirked over at the disguised Madeleine as he took his place back in the stands.

"Go on, Maud. Wipe that smirk off his greasy face," Edgar whispered from under his hood.

Alfie clutched his talisman for luck as Madeleine stepped up to the line. He was worried; his cousin had won many competitions in the past but there was a lot more riding on this contest, and she had never used Edgar's bow before. Alfie knew that it would be a good one, but no one could expect an archer to win a competition with an unfamiliar bow. He crossed his fingers tightly and held his breath.

The crowd was silent as Madeleine nocked another arrow then paused for a few seconds, sighting down the shaft at the target before releasing the arrow.

"Did she score?" Alfie squinted to see the target.

"Just," murmured Edgar from under his hood, "but she needs the next two to hit close to the centre now to even rank alongside Percy. Look at him, smirking."

Madeleine flexed her fingers then reached for another arrow, spending a little more time sighting the target.

"Are you sure she can't use her own bow?" asked Alfie. "I've got it right here in my bag."

"No, that would give us away," said Edgar. "She needs to use the same one I've used in all the stages of the contest so far."

Alfie held his breath as Madeleine let another arrow fly.

"Ooh, looking good," said Henry as the arrow whistled down the field.

The crowd burst into applause as it thudded into the target.

"She hit the centre?" Alfie gasped.

"The wooden peg right in the very centre!" cried Edgar, applauding with all his might. "She hit the nail right on the head! I've never managed that myself from that distance. Look, Percy's getting worried."

Percy did seem agitated. Alfie noticed that his knuckles were white as he sat in the stands clutching his bow. He didn't look like someone who was used to things not going his way. Alfie remembered the injuries to Edgar's arm and side and willed Madeleine to beat Percy.

"Come on, Maud," said Henry, bouncing on his toes.

"Shh!" said Edgar. "Remember, that's me up there!"

Madeleine nocked her final arrow. Her chest rose as she took a long, deep breath, held it as she sighted the target, then breathed out as she released the arrow.

"Come on, come on..." Alfie heard Edgar whisper.

There was a second of silence as the arrow sliced through the air, thudding into the target so close to the second that it stripped off some of its feathers. The crowd roared and leapt to its feet.

"She did it, she did it!" cried Henry over the thunderous applause.

"HE! You mean HE!" Edgar hissed in his ear.

"Ed-gar, Ed-gar!" chanted Henry, quickly.

Alfie saw Percy try, and fail, to snap his bow before throwing it to the ground and storming away from the field. He didn't appear used to losing.

Madeleine hurried over to them. "Quick, while they're confirming the scores." She grabbed Edgar and hurried behind the stands. Alfie and Henry stood side by side to hide them from view as Madeleine pulled Edgar's cloak over the fine clothes he had lent her. She put up her hood and passed him the chaperon hat.

"Thank you, all of you," said Edgar, shaking

hands with everyone as he emerged from behind the stands. His eyes shone as he bowed deeply to Madeleine. "You're a fine shot, Maud. I wish you could take the praise for it, but you have my eternal thanks, and my coach to take you anywhere you need to go. Is there anything else I can do for any of you?"

"Maybe one thing," said Alfie, looking down at Henry. The boy seemed very quiet now that his new friends were about to leave. "You wouldn't happen to need a groom? Henry here is wonderful with animals, and very quick to learn. If you gave him a job then we'd be more than square."

Edgar smiled. "As luck would have it, my father just bought two new horses from Barrett. I'm sure he'd appreciate another pair of hands for the stables."

Henry beamed. "Can I bring my dog, Stinker?" he begged. "He's a brilliant ratter, just what you need in the stables."

"I suppose a good ratter never goes amiss," said Edgar. Henry spat on his hand then held it out to Edgar, who recoiled in horror, then patted him on the shoulder. "You're hired, but no need to shake on it. Ever."

The targets and arrows had been checked and

the crowd had begun to chant, "Lum-ley, Lum-ley, Lum-ley." Alfie bowed and Madeleine gave a clumsy curtsey as Edgar bowed low then walked out to accept the cheers of the crowd and his reward.

"This is for you, Henry," said Alfie, tipping some of the silver coins from his pouch into the boy's hands. "You'll do a good job for Edgar, won't you?"

"Cross my heart and hope to die," said Henry, tucking the money very carefully into his shoes and various pockets. "I hope your friend gets better soon," he called after them as they hurried towards the coach that was waiting by Edgar's tent.

13

The Witch of Demon Rock

It was almost noon by the time the coach pulled up in front of the barn. The driver seemed a little bothered that he had been ordered to drive a bunch of peasants wherever they wanted to go, but had nodded curtly as Alfie had asked him to take them up to the islands near Bamburgh Castle.

"Where've you been?" exploded Robin as Alfie and Madeleine burst into the barn. "We need to leave now, the farmer will be back any min—" He stopped and stared in amazement as Madeleine threw back her cloak.

"Niiiice threads!" said Amy, looking Madeleine up and down as she posed proudly in Edgar's finery. "Don't tell me you've been off getting a makeover all this time?" Alfie suddenly realized they had left Madeleine's medieval clothing in Edgar's tent. He had a feeling that Madeleine didn't exactly forget to change back into her dress before they left. He hoped Edgar wouldn't mind that she hadn't given his clothes back, and wondered what he would think of her jeans.

"Maddie, your hair!" said Robin as she removed her cloak. "What did you *do*? Mum is going to kill you."

"We'll explain on the way," said Alfie, trying to delay revealing that he was the one who had cut Madeleine's hair. "Come on, help me with Bryn."

They each took a limb and hauled Bryn outside. Robin and Amy almost dropped him as they saw the coach standing there.

"Whoa, how did you afford this?" asked Robin as they pulled Bryn through the coach door. "Is it from Muninn and Bone?"

"Nope," said Alfie. "This is courtesy of a new friend, and it's all thanks to Madeleine."

The coach rumbled on its way and Alfie filled everyone in on Madeleine's triumph in the tournament as they shared the chicken, bread and apples he had bought at the castle. Madeleine chimed in to add fanciful details, describing how she had split an arrow from a hundred metres. Alfie could see that Robin longed to say that was impossible but even he was holding his tongue after Madeleine had saved the day for them all.

"You should have seen her, she was amazing," said Alfie. Madeleine blushed with pride at the praise.

"Well done, Maddie," said Robin. "We'll be there by tonight, all thanks to you." His eyes flicked to her hair. "But Mum is still going to kill you."

"Totally worth it," grinned Madeleine as Amy ruffled her cropped hair.

They began to doze off one by one as the coach rumbled on. Alfie watched the unconscious Bryn, who had been propped up in the seat opposite him. Madeleine checked his pulse and breathing now and then, but nothing had changed. Alfie hoped that Orin and Ashford weren't getting any worse either. He wished one of them had stayed behind at the castle to make sure they were OK, but knew that they wouldn't have stood a chance if the wraith had gone back there.

The wraith haunted the darkness behind Alfie's eyelids as he closed his eyes. It must have sensed the magic inside him when the rangers had taken his talisman. He instinctively reached up to check it was still hanging around his neck, but it didn't make him feel any safer. It was on their trail and, despite the protective talisman, Alfie worried that now it had their scent it would keep coming. He had weakened it temporarily, but he knew that it would be after them again once darkness fell. He wasn't sure he'd be able to hold it off when it came for them again, if he even saw it coming. They had to get to the witch before nightfall, before the wraith began hunting again.

The rocking motion of the coach lulled Alfie into uneasy dreams in which he was flying on Artan, only for the skies to darken and black clouds to stretch out long, grasping fingers that tried to snatch him out of the sky. He jerked awake as the coach bounced on an uneven track. Robin was sitting next to him, reading from one of Orin's books. Alfie watched his cousin's lips moving as he sounded out the strange runic writing.

"I don't know how you can read that," said Alfie, rubbing his eyes. "It makes no sense at all to me."

"It makes more sense since Orin ran through the basics with us," said Robin, marking his place with his finger. "And it's a lot easier if you use this key he created." He handed Alfie a sheet of parchment on which Orin had translated all of the symbols he had used.

"Oh, there's a key!" said Alfie, taking the parchment and pretending to study it. He didn't like to admit that he had already seen it and still hadn't managed to translate more than a few words. How could Orin expect him to learn to control the magic inside him as well as learning the medical applications of herbs AND the spells and knowledge in the books that filled his study? Alfie sighed as he handed the parchment back to Robin. Orin might as well have asked Madeleine or Robin to train with him. He was just a container – a hiding place for a magic Orin wanted to get rid of.

He leaned his face against the plush wall of the coach and stared out of the window. The forest on the left had given way to open countryside and on the right he could see the sea beyond the fields. The sky was darker than it should be for the time of year and tiny raindrops had begun to spatter the windows.

"Not long to go now," said Madeleine, from opposite him. "We passed Alnwick well over an hour ago. It was weird seeing the castle there. Mum and Dad took us there years ago and it looks just the same now, six hundred years in the past. I know it sounds daft, but it made me really homesick to see it."

"I know how you feel," said Alfie, thinking longingly of his own castle and wondering what his dad was doing as time passed in the future. Probably pottering around in his workshop, chasing Galileo out every now and then. Alfie wondered how much that future would change if they failed to cure Orin.

"Hey, sleepyhead," said Alfie as Amy sat up from where she had slumped against Bryn and stretched. "Any more premonitions?"

"Only if I'm going to be riding a winged snow leopard to school sometime soon," said Amy, scratching her armpit. "Man, I *hope* that was a premonition."

The raindrops splattering the window grew larger as the coach rolled on. Looking out to sea, Alfie could see white tips to the waves. No one said anything, but he knew that they were all thinking the same thing: what if the weather was too bad? What if no one would take them out to the island?

The coach finally rolled to a stop by a small harbour in which several fishing boats were moored. Sea birds wheeled screeching overhead.

Out among the cresting waves, Alfie could see several craggy islands. One of them had to be Demon Rock.

The harbour was empty apart from one man sitting in a boat mending nets. He looked up, eyes narrowed suspiciously as Alfie jumped down from the coach and hurried over the pebbled beach towards him.

"I hope you're not collecting taxes," he growled as Alfie reached the boat.

"I'm not after money, sir," said Alfie. "I was—"

"Cos I've had enough of you lot, sitting about in your big houses and castles, taking hard-earned money from us as can't well afford it."

"I promise I'm not here for taxes," said Alfie, avoiding mention of living in castles. "That coach isn't even mine. We're here because we need your help."

"Hmph." The fisherman looked Alfie up and down. "Well I guess you're not dressed like one of that lot, unless you've fallen on really hard times without honest folks' money to keep you in silks and pointy shoes. So what brings you to ask help of the likes of me on a night like this?"

"We need to get to Demon Rock. Can you take us?" asked Alfie. "We'll pay you."

The fisherman looked up at the thick black clouds as a distant rumble of thunder echoed across the bay. "Perhaps tomorrow afternoon, if the skies are clear by then. Come and see me in the morning, I'll let you know then."

"Tomorrow's no good," said Alfie. "We need to go now."

"Now?" The fisherman laughed as he tucked away the nets and jumped down from the boat. "You want me to sail you four miles out, when there's a storm on its way? I might be old, but I'm not mad. No, come and see me in the morning."

"Please," pleaded Alfie. "We've travelled all the way from Hexbridge and we *must* get to the island tonight. We can pay you." He handed over the pouch of silver coins. "Here. It's all we've got, but it's yours, *if* you take us now."

The fisherman's eyes bulged as he sifted through the contents of the pouch. He sat down hard on the jetty as if he didn't trust his legs to support him.

"That's a lot of money," he said, holding tightly on to the pouch as he stared up at the dark clouds. "A lot of money."

Alfie stood quietly, twisting the hem of his tunic as he watched the fisherman weighing up the value of the fare against the coming storm.

"Well, I can't say I've ever been known for my brains," he said at last. "I'll take you soon, but first I'd better tell the family I'll be late home."

"Thank you!" said Alfie. "Thank you so much."

"Not sure you'll be thanking me if you find yourself at the bottom of the sea," said the fisherman. "I'll take no more than two of you – that's the most I'll have on my conscience. The others can wait in one of them caves in the cliff. The tide never comes up that far."

Alfie hurried back to the coach to tell the others.

"Are you sure about going tonight?" asked Robin as rain pattered down softly around them. "The weather is going to get a lot worse before long."

"I know," said Alfie. "But what if it's bad for days? We can't wait. We've got to find the witch and get back to the castle." He looked from his cousins to Amy. One by one, they nodded in agreement. "Right then, we'd better get Bryn to one of those caves."

"We really appreciate you bringing us all this way." Alfie thanked the driver as they lifted Bryn down from the coach. "Would you mind. . ." But the driver shook the reins and the coach rumbled away before Alfie could ask if he would wait for them.

"I suppose we weren't specific about getting a lift back too," groaned Alfie as they hoisted Bryn up the beach and into a dry little cave littered with driftwood.

"I'll stay with Bryn," said Robin. "Madeleine, you should stay too in case he gets any worse."

"Not sure there's anything I'd be able to do," said Madeleine. "I'll stay, but what if the wraith comes for us? It'll be dark in a couple of hours."

"It's me it's after," said Alfie. "And if you light a fire at the mouth of the cave, it should leave you alone."

"I've been practising one of Orin's spells," said Robin. "I think it will help all of us. Quick, before the fisherman gets back, show me his boat."

Madeleine and Amy laid a circle of stones at the entrance to the cave and began to fill it with driftwood as Alfie took Robin down to the boat. Robin placed his hands on the wood and closed his eyes. His brow furrowed in concentration as he began to recite something under his breath. It might have been a trick of the light, but Alfie could swear that for a brief second he saw a golden web encase the whole boat as Robin staggered back from it, breathing hard.

"Protection spell," he panted as Alfie grabbed

his arm to support him. "Took a bit more effort than I thought, but it should keep you safe from the worst of the wind and waves. I can cast the same spell across the mouth of the cave, though I doubt the wraith will be able to travel so well in this wind."

Amy and Madeleine already had a fire blazing by the cave when they returned.

"Are you sure about coming with me?" Alfie asked Amy as she got up and brushed the sand from her tunic.

"I saved you from drowning in the lake last half-term, didn't I?" she said. "You'll be safer with me on board."

"And are you both going to be all right here?" he asked Madeleine and Robin as they made themselves comfortable next to Bryn.

"Don't worry about us. We'll be fine," said Robin.

"Just come back safely, OK?" said Madeleine, getting up to give Alfie and Amy a hug. "Now go on, before he leaves without you."

Alfie could hear Robin begin to cast the lilting chant of protection over the cave entrance as he hurried down to the shore with Amy. The fisherman had untied the boat and was pushing it down to the sea. A young man was helping him.

From their similar craggy features, Alfie guessed it was the man's son.

"Give me a hand," he shouted over the whistling wind.

Alfie put his shoulder to the boat alongside Amy and they heaved it into the water. The fisherman and his son leapt on board and reached down to hoist Alfie and Amy up on to the boat as it bobbed about in the choppy water.

"Wish we'd brought our wellies," groaned Amy as water squelched out of their soft leather boots.

"Put these on," grunted the fisherman, throwing them a stiff heavy cape each. "Oilskins."

Alfie pulled his over his head, too grateful for the waterproof garment to object to its rancid smell.

The storm was starting to build as they sailed out of the tiny harbour and into the open sea. The fisherman was steering the boat with a wooden tiller at the back. His son was looking after the taut sail, which was driving them swiftly through the water in the high winds. The waves grew larger the further out they travelled. Each time the boat bounced over a particularly large one, Alfie and Amy were thrown into the air to come crashing back down on to the hard wooden bench.

Alfie's teeth clattered together painfully each time. However, as much as the waves and the wind played with the little boat, it stayed on course and kept on pushing forward. Alfie was sure he saw a wave that should have splashed over into the boat glance off as though it had hit an invisible barrier. Robin's protection spell was working.

"Nice one, Robin," Alfie whispered as the boat forged a path through the waves.

It was getting quite dark now, but Alfie could see a large island looming on their left. A few lights twinkled from it. "Is that it?" he called over the roar of the sea.

"No, that's where the monks live," shouted the fisherman. "Demon Rock is the rocky island further out!"

His son whipped around, his eyes wild.

"You didn't tell me they were going to Demon Rock," he yelled as the wind blew his oilskin out around him. "You know I won't go near that place!"

"Now lad, don't start with that talk again. If a woman chooses to live wild with the birds and seals it don't mean she's a witch, just a bit odd in the head."

"But John Thatcher said—"

"John Thatcher don't have a brain in that skull of his, don't let him take yours too. Now, not a word more. These folks here paid well for passage to Demon Rock, and that's where we're taking them."

Alfie could sense the tension between father and son as the boat sped on. A flash of lightning illuminated the sky for a second, and they all leapt at a roar of thunder, like the crack of a dozen cannons. Alfie held tightly on to the side of the boat with one hand and was grateful when Amy linked his other arm with hers. Her dark hair was plastered across her face with salt water and her skin was a pale bluish-green.

"Seasick yet?" she asked as the boat smacked down on the other side of a large wave.

Alfie gave a half smile, not daring to open his mouth to answer as his stomach churned like the sea. He tried closing his eyes briefly, but not knowing whether a wave was going to come crashing down over them was even worse.

"Land ahoy, starboard side!" shouted the fisherman. A flash of lightning illuminated a jagged mass of rocks on their right as the thunder rolled around them. Large pillars towered out of the waves like giant chimney stacks. "There's an area where we can land a little way around," he yelled over the dying roar. "Be ready to jump out. We can't stay too close for long or we'll be dashed to pieces on the rocks."

Alfie stared at the island. It was little more than a large outcrop of rocky columns clustered together to form an island on which huddled more seabirds than Alfie had ever seen in his life – puffins, gulls, gannets and many more he couldn't name all huddled in among the rocks, watching the boat skirting around their island.

They finally pulled into a tiny inlet where the waves weren't as fierce.

"Hop out there," said the fisherman, pulling alongside a low section of rock. Alfie clambered out of the rocking boat on to the slippery rocks and reached out to help Amy. The fisherman's son stayed at the far end of the boat, as if he'd be forever cursed just by touching the island. Just as Amy leapt to join Alfie, there was a blinding flash. A jagged bolt of lightning cut through the air to strike the boat's mast. As it struck, Alfie saw a faint shimmer, like a burst of gold dust, as the protection Robin had cast over the boat was dispelled.

The boat and the fishermen were unharmed, but the second the protection disappeared they were fully at the mercy of the wind and waves as the boat pitched and rolled, knocking against the rocks.

"Sorry, lad, but it's too dangerous for us to stay here," called the fisherman over the crashing waves as he began to steer the boat back out to sea. "We need to leave! We'll moor her over on the monks' island. You hole up somewhere dry – we'll be back to get you tomorrow!"

Alfie watched the boat bouncing away on the churning sea. They were alone on Demon Rock with only the wind and the watchful eyes of the island's avian guardians.

"What now?" asked Amy, shivering alongside him.

"We find the witch," said Alfie.

They had to be very careful where they put their hands as they climbed up the slippery rocks. There seemed to be a nest of snapping beaks in every niche.

"Ow," yelped Amy as a gull snapped at her fingers for the third time. "It wouldn't be so bad if we could actually see where we were going."

"I might be able to help," said Alfie, reaching deep down to the ancient magic inside him and feeling a small scrap of remaining energy from the fire it had fed on the night before. He concentrated it towards his chest and the talisman lens began to glow, like a small torch lighting their way.

"Urgh, not sure if that was a good idea after all," said Amy, wrinkling her nose as she examined the gooey white substance coating the rocks they were clambering over. Alfie tried not to think about the slimy bird droppings under his fingers as they hauled themselves the rest of the way up on to the island.

The wind was fierce and Alfie had to crouch low, oilskin hood pulled tightly around his face to keep out the rain as they staggered over the rocky island.

"Watch out for holes!" he yelled to Amy as he slipped in the sandy soil between the rocks and got his foot stuck in a burrow.

"Puffins," he panted to Amy as she wrapped her arm around his back for support. He pulled himself free and rubbed his ankle. "Robin said they have burrows all over the island."

"Where to now?" asked Amy. They stayed huddled together for warmth as Alfie turned slowly, the narrow beam of light from his talisman highlighting the pillars of rock around the island from which large seabirds shook out their wings threateningly.

"What's that, up there?" said Amy suddenly.

Alfie turned the light back to the highest point of the island where a ramshackle building was defying the elements against all odds.

"I guess that's where she lives," shivered Alfie. "Come on, maybe she'll have a fire."

The light from the talisman began to fade as they picked their way over the green rocks to a tumbledown cottage. It had been built from rocks and driftwood stacked carefully together, almost as if the builder had approached its creation like a bird or animal making a nest or burrow. A broken section of a boat's hull formed the roof. The whole structure had been built against a rocky shelf, which gave it some protection from the wind.

"Hello?" called Alfie as he knocked loudly on the wooden walls. "Is anyone in there?" There was no response. He walked around the side to search for a door and found a smaller overturned boat. It was mostly rotten. He leaned over to look through one of the jagged holes, and a large yellow-and-orange beak shot out and snapped at his nose. Alfie leapt back at the loud squawking of an entire family of puffins and hit his head on something hard. He turned and fell backwards with a yell as a white face loomed out of the darkness.

"What is it?" shouted Amy, dashing to his side

as the talisman lit up an eerie figure, half fish, half woman, expressionless eyes staring fixedly at them.

Alfie flinched as Amy punched him in the arm.

"It's just a figurehead from the front of a ship. You nearly gave me a heart attack, Al!"

Alfie stared up at the wooden figure as he rubbed his arm. It had been built into the side of the cottage. The witch had an interesting sense of humour. He stooped and shone his talisman through a gap that might have served for a window. He could barely see anything in the talisman's dying light, but could tell there was no one in there. A large cooking pot sat in the centre of the room, and in the corner was a mat woven from dried sea grass that might have served as a bed, but it didn't look as though anyone had been there in quite a while.

"Give me a hand with this," said Amy, pulling at an iron-studded door that might once have been the door to a ship's cabin.

Alfie grasped the handle and pulled with Amy, but it wouldn't budge an inch.

A loud barking suddenly carried over the wind.

"What was that?" said Alfie, whipping around.

"It came from over there," said Amy as more and

more barks filled the air. She grasped Alfie by the shoulders and turned him so that the talisman's light shone down to the sea.

"Seals!" gasped Alfie as a dozen of them leapt out of the waves and on to the island.

"Do you think they're dangerous?" asked Amy as the baying creatures advanced towards them.

"Yes, I do," said Alfie, remembering a nature programme he had seen in which male seals were fighting, savaging each other with their sharp teeth. As more and more seals heaved themselves out of the water the light from the talisman finally died completely, leaving them in darkness. Over the wind, Alfie could hear the slapping of the seals, bodies on the rocks as they dragged themselves closer, barking like a pack of dogs.

Clutching Amy's arm, Alfie backed away only to hear more seals approaching from behind them. He staggered over a rock and stopped still; it was too dangerous to run across the craggy, burrow-filled island in the dark. Without the light to guide them they could break their legs or run straight off a cliff into the thrashing waves. If only there was something he could draw energy from to create more light. *Oh, but there is*, whispered the magic harboured deep inside him. He could feel it pushing him from within, urging him to reach out to the seals, to let it feed on their life energy and use it to create something to drive them away. *It's them or you,* it whispered as he backed up against the little hut and pulled at the door with Amy.

The wild musky smell of the seals was all around them now. The roar of the wind and waves and the baying of the seals rang through his ears, competing with the whispering in his head and the ravenous hunger of the magic inside him. It was all too much for Alfie.

"Stop!" he screamed into the wind as he whirled around clutching his head. "Just *STOP!*" He fell back against the door and sank to the ground. The seals were suddenly silent.

"What did you do?" asked Amy, crouching down beside him.

"Nothing," said Alfie, looking up. "At least I don't think I did."

A bolt of lightning lit up the whole sky and Alfie's breath caught in his throat. A woman was standing among the seals and they had all turned to gaze up at her.

"Did you see that?" he whispered to Amy as the light flickered away, followed by a low rumble. "Where did she come from?" Amy didn't answer but by the way she pressed herself back against the door he knew she had seen her too.

A hoarse voice chanted something and a remarkable change came over the island. Every tiny rock-pool, each piece of seaweed and scrap of moss began to glow in greens, blues and purples. It was as though the whole island had become some amazing deep-sea creature. Lit by the gentle glow of the island itself the woman walked towards them, her pale wet skin reflecting the colours of the mysterious lights. Her long hair hung down before her, wet and straggly like seaweed. Alfie couldn't even guess at her age; she looked neither old nor young. He knew this had to be the person they had travelled so far to find. The witch of Demon Rock.

"Why did you come here?" she rasped slowly, as though trying to remember how to talk. Alfie sensed thousands of eyes on them as every bird and seal on the island watched the exchange. "What do you want?" she demanded, stopping before them.

"Help," Alfie managed to splutter. "We need your help."

"Help," she spat, eyes flashing with anger. "Of course you need help. On land they all hate or fear me, yet when things turn bad they all want my help. I came here to be alone and yet you follow

236

me. No, you will leave my island. You people must learn to help yourselves."

"It's not for us," said Alfie, scrambling out of the way as the witch strode towards her cottage and traced a symbol on the door with her finger. It sprang open and she went inside. "It's for a friend – I think you know him too. Orin Hopcraft."

The witch froze, halfway through closing the door.

"You know the great druid?" she asked, eyes narrowed. "You are friends of his?"

"Yes!" said Alfie. "Something bad has happened to him. The last thing he wrote was this message." He pulled Orin's crumpled note from his tunic and handed it to her. "He wanted us to come and find you. I think only you can help him."

She was silent for a moment then nodded and opened the door to them.

Alfie paused for a moment, then followed her inside.

14

No Ordinary Wolves

It was clear the witch hadn't had visitors before. She seemed to have forgotten the need for light or even heat. It wasn't until she noticed Alfie and Amy huddling together, teeth chattering as they squinted to see through the gloom, that she thought to light the fire in the pit at the centre of the hut.

"Thank you," said Alfie as he took off his oilskin and wet boots and shuffled closer to the fire.

"What's that for?" asked Amy warily as the witch set up a small cauldron over the fire.

"Soup. Mostly," said the witch, unstopping a bottle and pouring water into the pot, followed by a large pinch of something with an aromatic and savoury smell from a jar. She reached up for some of the strips of dried meat hanging on a string that ran from one side of the hut to the other. "Rabbit," she said, tearing the meat into smaller pieces and adding them to the pot. "Makes a nice change from fish." She smiled at them for the first time and Alfie was surprised at the sudden warmth in her features.

"Er ... do you think you could..." he began, cheeks flaming red. "Um, I mean, would you mind..."

"What's wrong with him?" asked the witch.

"Um, maybe you could put some clothes on?" said Amy delicately.

The witch looked down as though the thought hadn't even occurred to her. She grabbed a long, dark green cloak hanging from a nail and wrapped it around herself, before ladling portions of the bubbling rabbit stew into white-and-blue patterned bowls. They were encrusted with barnacles as if they had come from a shipwreck.

Alfie raised the bowl to slurp the stew in an attempt to cover his flaming red cheeks. It was better than he expected; he could feel the warming spices travel right down into his stomach to heat him from the inside out.

"Now," said the witch, the flames casting dancing shadows across her face. "Tell me what has befallen Orin Hopcraft."

Over two helpings of stew Alfie and Amy poured out the story of the wraith and what it had done to the people of Miggleswick, Ashford and Orin himself. They told of how it had followed them and marked Bryn, draining him of life.

"For all we know it might be heading here right now," said Alfie.

"Small streams might not slow it much," said the witch. "But a creature like that will not be able to travel across the sea. It will wait for you, though, and it will not stop until it has what it wants – the magic hidden inside you."

Alfie felt as though he had just had an electric shock. "What do you mean?" he asked feebly. How did she know about the magic? He had avoided mentioning it throughout the entire tale, but the witch's eyes seemed to look right through him.

"You are him," said the witch. "The boy chosen by the Sisters of Fate to harbour powerful magic." She smiled at Alfie as he fought for something to say. "Even if the druid had not told me of this plan, I would have known that there was such a thing inside you. I could feel its hunger as it turned its gaze on my friends."

"The seals," whispered Alfie. "You know what it wanted me to do? I'm . . . I'm sorry."

"Why sorry?" asked the witch. "Despite your fear, you did not act on its desire. You are strong, Alfie Bloom. The Fates chose well."

"You know my name, and this is my friend, Amy Siu. So what's your name?" asked Alfie. "We can't keep calling you 'the Witch'."

She laughed. "I've been called worse. I am Fionnuala – but you may call me Nuala. Now, rest while I prepare for the trip. The sea has many healing gifts that I must gather before we leave."

Alfie sighed as he settled down into the sea-grass next to Amy. He had hoped to leave straight away, but the little boat that must have belonged to the witch was no longer seaworthy. Though the storm was passing he knew the fishermen wouldn't be back for many hours. Nuala must have been trapped alone on the island for years. He closed his eyes, praying that Robin, Madeleine and Bryn were safe in their little cave on the beach.

"Time to go." Alfie felt Nuala shake his shoulder and groaned as he sat up. Amy was already up and pulling on her boots by the glowing embers of the fire. It was still dark outside. "What time is it?" he asked.

"Still a few hours till dawn," said the witch. "But the storm has calmed enough for us to leave."

"The boat won't be back until the morning," said Alfie. "How can we leave?"

"With help from some friends of mine," said Nuala. "When you're ready, bring those sacks and meet me down by the water, where you first saw the seals."

With that she wrenched the door from its hinges and disappeared into the night. Alfie could hear her dragging the door behind her as he pulled on his boots and strapped one of the sacks across his back.

"What did she take the door for?" asked Amy.

Alfie pulled the oilskin cape back over his clothes. "Let's go and find out."

The rain was no longer pouring so heavily and the storm was starting to die down. Alfie could hear very faint rumbles far in the distance but the moon was out from behind the clouds and shone brightly down on the water. The magical coloured lights that had lit the island were fading away, but it was easy to find their way in the moonlight. Nuala was crouched by rocks down by the water, tying knots in long lengths of rope. As they got closer the rocks moved and Alfie realized she was surrounded by seals.

"Hush!" said the witch as the seals began to bark again. She beckoned to Alfie and Amy and pointed to her front door that was now lying in the sand. "Your raft. Climb aboard." She had tied several lengths of rope around the door and trailed them out on the sand in front of it. She patted one of the knots she had made at intervals in the rope. "For the seals to bite on to," she said. "They will tow you safely to shore."

"What about you?" asked Amy as they climbed aboard the raft and lay down on their stomachs. "There's only enough room for me and Alfie."

"I'm going to swim," said Nuala, making loops of rope for them to hang on to and to hook their feet through. She shed her cloak, tucked it under Amy's oilskin and stepped into the sea.

"You can't swim back!" Alfie cried. "It's miles, and the water's ice cold. You'll freeze."

"I'll be just fine," she smiled. "Now hold on tight, we'll try to make it as smooth a ride as possible."

"We?" Alfie mouthed to Amy, but she was staring straight ahead, her mouth open in a little "o". Alfie followed her gaze to the witch. "Whoa," he whispered under his breath. As Nuala walked into the water her body was transforming. A mottled pattern seemed to be spreading across the pale skin of her back and upper arms, her nose and mouth elongated into a muzzle and her eyes shone pure black. With a graceful leap she dived forward into the sea. Seconds later a seal surfaced in exactly the same spot.

"Did that really just happen?" whispered Amy, her eyes shining as they watched the other seals slip into the water after Nuala.

"She's a selkie," gasped Alfie. "They're human on land, and seals in the water. Granny has loads of stories about them."

Nuala was easy to spot among the other seals: she was larger, and pale – almost silver. She barked to the other seals and they each took one of the knots in their jaws. Alfie grasped the rope handholds tightly as their makeshift raft was dragged into the sea. Seconds later they were flying across the water, bouncing over the waves as the seals sped towards the shore.

Alfie's fear that they would be thrown off into the sea soon gave way to exhilaration as the wind blew back his hair. It was almost as much fun as travelling on Artan, but colder, and much wetter.

The sea spray caught their faces as the seals jostled each other to take turns at towing the raft.

"Woo!" yelled Amy.

"Wooo!" Alfie joined in, and the cries whipped from his mouth as he yelled into the wind.

"There's the boat," he shouted, pointing to what the fisherman had called the Monks' Island. He was very relieved to see they had made it to safety in the storm without Robin's protection spell. "I wonder what they'll think when they go back to Demon Rock and see we're not there?"

"Nuala sent one of the puffins to the island with a note while you were asleep," Amy shouted back. "It told them not to bother going back for us. She signed it *The Witch*, so they'll probably think she ate us." She grinned. "I like her."

The journey back was so much quicker than the voyage to the island. The seals cut through the water at incredible speed. It wasn't long before Alfie saw the silhouette of the little houses near the beach where they had left the twins and Bryn. Squinting through the gloom he could make out the distant light of the fire in the cave mouth. He gave a little sigh of relief as he pointed it out to Amy. If the fire was still lit then the others must be safe.

"Head for that light!" he shouted to Nuala. She bobbed her head and the craft turned slightly to head straight towards the beach.

Alfie felt a coldness grip his stomach as they drew closer to shore. He scanned the beach. Would the wraith be waiting for them in the shadows?

Leaping to his feet the second the raft scraped on to the shore Alfie called out his thanks to the seals and ran up the beach towards the cave. It must have been around five o'clock and the early dawn light was starting to spill on to the sand.

Robin was sitting at the mouth of the cave feeding the fire. He jumped to his feet as he saw Alfie coming. Madeleine was dozing, propped up against Bryn as though he was a giant cushion. She woke with a start as Alfie skidded into the cave.

"Did you find her?" Robin asked, before Alfie could say a word. "Did you find the witch?" He looked pale and very tired. Alfie suspected he had stayed awake all night to make sure his spell worked.

"We did," said Alfie. "She's down there with Amy."

"Down there?" cried Madeleine, clambering to her feet. "Get them up here quick!"

"What's wrong?" asked Alfie as Robin grabbed his arm and began to run back down the beach.

"It's here – the wraith. It's been gliding up and down the beach all night, like it sensed you'd been here. It wasn't too interested in us, and the fire and protection spell stopped it from coming too close, but it could be back any minute. We've got to get everyone into the cave."

Alfie and Robin pounded down the beach to where they had pulled ashore. He could see Nuala, now back in her human form and pulling on a long green dress. Amy was waving off the seals as they set out to return the witch's front door to the island. Out of the corner of his eye, Alfie saw a dark shape detach itself from the shadow of the boats.

"Amy, Nuala, look out!" he screamed as it moved swiftly towards them. They turned and Nuala pushed Amy behind her as she saw the wraith – but it had stopped at Alfie's shout. Alfie stopped dead in his tracks as it turned and began to glide over the sand towards him.

"Run, Alfie. Run!" screamed Robin, scrambling back towards the cave, but Alfie's legs wouldn't move. He looked frantically about him. Maybe he could drive it away with light and wind again? But he couldn't see anything to draw energy from, only sand, rocks and water – Robin's fire was too far away. *What about your friends?* whispered the magic. *You could borrow from them.* He tried to shake the horrific suggestion from his mind as he willed his legs to move, but it was too late: he fell back into the sand and shielded his face as the wraith loomed over him and lowered a long wispy finger down towards his chest.

Alfie screamed in agony and dropped to the ground as the finger disappeared into his body; it felt as though an icicle had pierced his heart. He could hear every one of the wraith's voices in his head, young and old all screaming out for the magic inside him, the magic that would let them return to the grave once they passed it to their master. Was this how Bryn and Orin had felt as the wraith had drained the life from them? But he knew it wasn't life that the wraith wanted from him. Electricity jolted through Alfie's veins as the magic inside him began to flow towards the wraith.

Alfie heard himself screaming again, but as soon as the sensation had started, it stopped. The intense icy pain eased as the wraith pulled away from him. He clutched his chest, rolled over on to his knees, and was sick on the sand. Someone was chanting and he was aware of a commotion around him, but he sat there panting, eyes closed as warmth gradually returned to his chest.

"Al, it's OK," said Amy, sitting down in the sand next to him and gripping him around the shoulders. "Nuala got it away from you."

With the help of Amy and Robin, Alfie staggered to his feet. Madeleine had run down the beach to join them. The wraith was floating just above their heads, roiling furiously like angry black smoke trapped in a bubble.

"Can you get rid of it?" Alfie panted. He held on tightly to Amy and Robin's shoulders, not trusting his legs to support him after the attack.

"The spell that bonds it to its purpose is strong," said Nuala, moving her arms through the air in complicated patterns as though weaving a web. "I cannot destroy it or turn it from its path; I can only bind it for a time. We must move quickly." She finished her spell, pulled on her cloak and picked up the sack Amy had carried for her. "Where are your horses?" she asked.

"We don't have any," said Amy. "And we used the last of our money to pay for the trip to your island."

"No horses, no money," said Nuala, hands

resting on her hips. "Then we must be creative. Alfie, come with me. The rest of you, find a cart. There will be one close by that the fishermen use."

Alfie hurried alongside Nuala as she headed for the place where the woods trailed down towards the harbour.

"How are you?" she asked.

"OK, I think," said Alfie. "Thank you for saving me from that thing."

"You're not safe yet, but if we move fast we may have time to travel back to Hexbridge and prepare for your next encounter with it."

The thought of another encounter with the wraith made Alfie feel sick again, but he pressed his lips together and breathed deeply until the feeling passed.

At the edge of the woods, Nuala stopped and began to sing. Alfie didn't understand the words, but the song spoke to something deep within him, drawing him towards her. He realized it must be a spell, a summoning song, but what was she calling? His question was answered as something came crashing through the undergrowth.

Alfie backed away slowly as an enormous wolf burst out of the forest and padded over to stand before the witch. Alfie stared as she knelt and pressed her forehead against the wolf's. They stayed like that for a moment, silently communicating, then Nuala stood and the wolf threw back its head and howled. Half a dozen more wolves silently emerged from the forest at its call.

"They won't harm you," said Nuala. "They're here to help."

Alfie believed her, but kept a respectful distance as the wolves padded down on to the beach with them.

The wraith was still down by the shore, thrashing violently against the sphere Nuala had confined it to. Amy and the twins had found a cart and dragged it up the beach to the cave where Bryn lay.

"It was full of barrels that must have held fish," said Robin. "We unloaded them, but it still stinks a bit."

"Are those dogs?" said Madeleine, rushing towards the wolves sitting a small distance away. She stopped before she reached them and stared up at Nuala. "Wolves?" she gasped. "Why are they here?"

"They're going to take us to Orin," said Nuala, grabbing rope from a fishing boat and beginning to harness the wolves to the cart. Her eyes glanced to the wraith. "The holding spell won't last long – we need to hurry." Alfie could see that the orb confining the wraith was no longer a perfect sphere. It was becoming more and more misshapen as the creature struggled to free itself.

Alfie and Amy hurried into the cave. With the help of the twins they heaved Bryn across the sand and up on to the cart.

"Ready?" said Nuala as the twins and Amy jumped into the back of the cart with Bryn. There was no more room in the back, so Alfie climbed up to sit on the wooden bench at the front alongside the witch. The wolves were whining and pawing the ground, ready to go.

"I don't know about taking this cart," said Alfie. "Someone might need it. Maybe I could try to use the magic to create something like it?"

"I'll see that it is returned," said Nuala. "It is not wise for you to use your magic now, and I doubt you can create something resilient enough for this journey." With that she tossed back her head and let out a howl, and they were off. The wolves fought to find traction on the sand, but once their paws hit more solid ground the speed at which they moved was incredible.

"The wraith, it's getting free!" called Madeleine. Alfie looked over his shoulder just as the wraith burst out of its prison. A second later it disappeared from view as the wolves bounded into the woods.

"The sun is nearly up," said the witch. "It will follow, but it won't catch us."

The forest grew more and more dense as the wolves led them deeper, but they didn't slow down. Alfie wondered how they were going to keep going, but something strange was happening to the trees as they passed through. He had to look hard to figure out what it was, but then he stared in stunned silence as he realized. It was the forest itself. It seemed to be warping out of their way just briefly enough for them to pass through. At no point did they have to slow or go around anything; the wolves just kept running in a straight line.

"Are you doing this?" he asked Nuala.

"That would be telling," she said, passing the reins over to him. "Take over while I examine your friend."

"Wait, how?" he asked as she climbed over into the back of the cart to look at Bryn.

"There's nothing to it," she called back. "Just sit there. Don't interfere and leave the steering to the girls – they know where they're going."

Alfie felt a little useless at the front on his own with nothing to do. The reins that would allow him to steer the wolf at the head of the pack rested loosely in his lap as he tried to avoid looking straight ahead. The journey through the trees made him feel as though he was looking through a sphere of glass that was bending reality, and the wolves were travelling far too fast to even be possible.

Minutes later they burst out of the forest and were racing across the moors and hills. Even the rocks and heather seemed to warp out of the wolves' path. The sun was up now and cast a golden glow on everything but the wolves, which still looked as though they were bathed in moonlight. *These are no ordinary wolves*, Alfie thought to himself. He was glad they were travelling off the beaten track so the only attention their strange mode of transport attracted was from startled hares and crows.

"Well, there's life in him for a few days yet," said Nuala, climbing back over into the front. "Which is good news for Orin and the others, but we must move fast. The wraith will reach the castle tonight, and you, Alfie Bloom, must face it yourself if your friends are to be saved."

15

To Arms

As the sun rose high in the sky, the landscape began to look much more familiar to Alfie. Before long they were speeding through Hexbridge Forest, out the other side and into the village. The few people who saw them stared for a moment, then nodded and went on their way as the cart headed up the hill towards the castle. Alfie guessed they must have seen a few strange visitors to Orin's castle over the years, not least Alfie's parents, who had been dragged through time for him to be born here in the past.

Nuala had said little more on how Alfie was to face the wraith, only that he would have until around midnight to prepare. As they reached the castle he leapt out and lowered the drawbridge with the secret handle Bryn had shown him. The cart rattled over it and into the courtyard. Shaking off their harnesses, the wolves padded over to drink from the gargoyle fountain before dropping to the grass, panting gently. Alfie felt like lying down with them to rest in the summer sun.

Lifting Bryn from the cart, they laid him on a bed of hay in the stable alongside Betsy, then took Nuala up to see Orin in his study. He was just as they had left him, lying as though asleep in his armchair with the blanket they had tucked around him still in place. She took his cool hand in hers and pressed her forehead to his, just as she had done with the wolf.

"I am here," Alfie heard her whisper. "And I will bring you home."

She took the sack she had brought from the island and pulled out a variety of different sea plants, many of which Alfie had never seen before. She laid them out on the table by the window then scanned Orin's shelves, nodding as if happy with the herbs, powders and strange roots she saw there.

"Time for you to rest," she said, turning to Alfie, Amy and the twins.

"But you said the wraith is on its way here," said Alfie. "How can I prepare to face it if I'm asleep?"

"You already have everything you need to face it, except food and rest. You can't hope to succeed if you do not have your full strength. I will make preparations of my own, but tonight, you alone can save your friends."

Nuala brewed a soothing herbal tea to help them to sleep. Alfie took a shower before going to bed. As the warm water washed the sea salt from his hair and the mud from his legs, he thought of the wraith. How was he supposed to face it if even Orin had fallen victim to it? He couldn't yet do much with the magic hidden inside him. Robin had mastered spells far better than he could ever hope to, Madeleine knew just what to do when it came to healing wounds and creating medicines and salves, and even Amy had some strange ability that had warned her of the wraith's coming. What could he do? He had managed to drive the wraith away once, but he couldn't hope to stop it on his own.

Robin was already asleep by the time Alfie returned to their bedroom. Closing the curtains to shut out the afternoon light, he fell into a fitful sleep in which his bed seemed to rock as though being thrashed around on the waves. It seemed only moments before Madeleine gently shook him awake, but he felt better for the rest. He looked at Robin's travel clock by his bedside. It was just after six o'clock. Being summer it was still light outside, but it would get dark soon without the streetlights of the future bathing the village in their glow.

"Nuala said you should eat this," said Madeleine, thrusting a wooden bowl into his lap. "Salt pork and beans. It's really nice."

"Where's Robin?" asked Alfie, shuffling up in bed and taking a spoonful of the stew – it was good.

"Lighting the beacons on the towers and castle walls with Amy. Nuala asked them to. I've been up for a while collecting herbs and helping her brew a revitalizing potion. She said it will strengthen Orin and Bryn once you've saved them."

Alfie nearly choked on a mouthful of stew. "Saved them?" he coughed. "How am I supposed to do that if I don't even know what she wants me to do? How can she expect me to face that thing?"

"You faced it in the barn," said Madeleine gently. "We might all be like Bryn now if you hadn't done that."

"Yes, but all that did was drive it away for a little

while. It came back – I can't actually stop it. What was the point of going all that way to find the witch if I have to face it myself anyway?"

"Perhaps to learn that you have the strength to face it," said a voice from the doorway. Alfie's face flushed as he realized Nuala had overheard him.

"I'm sorry," he stammered. "I just. . ."

"When you are ready, come down to the Great Hall."

"Do you think she's angry?" Alfie whispered to Madeleine as Nuala walked away. She shook her head.

"I trust her, Alfie. She thinks you can do this, and we all know you can. You just need to have more faith in yourself."

Amy, Robin and Nuala had just finished lighting the fire in the Great Hall when Alfie and Madeleine made their way downstairs. Orin, Ashford and Bryn had been laid out in the centre of the room, hands folded on their chests and eyes closed. Despite the roaring fire, a coldness gripped Alfie as he stared at them lying like that. He felt as though he was at a wake.

"They are still alive, aren't they?" he asked.

Nuala nodded. "The wraith left them in a state between life and death."

"Why?" asked Alfie. The question had been bothering him for some time. "Why leave them only just alive when it could have killed them?"

"Because it's not evil, Alfie. It borrowed from them to feel whole again."

"And you don't think that's evil?" said Alfie. "That thing tracked us all the way on our journey to find you. It did this to Bryn, and you saw what it did to me when it tried to take the magic on the beach." He shuddered at the memory of its icy finger piercing his chest.

"Which is more cruel, the dog that bites, or the owner that starves and beats it and forces it to fight?"

"So what are you saying?" asked Alfie, a little spark igniting inside him. "I shouldn't blame the poor innocent wraith for what it did? I shouldn't fight it?" He waved his arm at Orin, Bryn and Ashford. "What about them? I thought you said I had to face it to save them."

"And face it you must, but there is a difference between facing and fighting. Remember who your real enemy is – the one forcing the wraith to do his bidding, the one who sent it after your magic."

"But how am I supposed to find him?"

"You won't have to," said Nuala. "He will come here tonight, with the wraith, I am sure of it. He will know it has found the magic, and will want to be here to receive it when the wraith takes it from you. But that's not going to happen," she added, seeing Alfie's ashen face. "You are going to use the magic to take back the life it has stolen. You told me you have drawn energy from flames, so you will draw the life the wraith has stolen in just the same way. Only then will it be weak enough for me to break the curse that binds it together."

"But how?" asked Alfie. "How am I supposed to do that when it's trying to take the magic from me? It hurt so much when it attacked me, I couldn't even think!"

"You can do it, Alfie," said Nuala, her dark eyes fixed on his. "We'll be by your side. I will help to bind it."

"And I'll perform Orin's protection spell," said Robin.

"This should help too," said Madeleine, holding up a small cauldron of steaming green liquid with a very strong herbal and seaweedy smell. "I helped Nuala make it. It's a strengthening potion. Not for muscle strength, but it will help us to fight back if it tries to do to us what it did to Orin and Bryn.

Here…" She dipped a cup into the liquid and handed it to Alfie. "Drink some."

The pungent steam from the cup was making his eyes water so Alfie held his nose and gulped down the liquid. For a second it felt as though the potion had surged through every vein in his body and set them on fire, but then the sensation eased to a gentle warmth in his stomach and chest, as though there was a small candle burning inside him.

"What *was* that?" he gasped as Madeleine took back the cup.

"The protection of the land and sea," said Nuala. "One of my favourite potions, made even more powerful with Madeleine's help. She's a natural herbalist, a witch of strong potential if ever I met one."

The others gasped too as one by one they took a draught of the potion. Alfie felt better than he had in days. He felt strong, but would he be strong enough? The thought of the wraith coming sent the flame inside him flickering in the cold draught of fear.

"How will we know when it's near?" he asked. "Amy, you had those dreams about it. Is there any way you can see it while you're awake?"

The colour drained from Amy's face as she stared at him. "I'm not sure. Maybe. I've tried not to think about it since those dreams. It was like I could see through its eyes, hear all the voices inside it. . . It was terrible."

"I know. I heard them too when it attacked me. That was terrifying enough, so I can't even imagine being inside its head." He squeezed her arm. "You don't have to do it, not if you don't want to."

The side of her mouth turned up in a weak smile. "Everyone else is doing something. If this is my way of helping, I'll do it. I'm just not sure how."

"I will aid you, child," said Nuala, drawing a small vial from her robe. She pulled out a large chair and indicated for Amy to sit down. "Now, close your eyes." Nuala shook a silvery droplet of liquid from the vial on to her finger and smeared it across Amy's eyelids. "This will help you to see."

"Are you sure about this, Amy?" Alfie asked.

"Yes." Amy leaned back into the chair and began to breathe deeply.

Alfie sat beside her, sharing glances with the twins as they watched Amy in silence, listening to her steady breathing. After about a minute her eyelids began to flicker and her fingers gripped the arms of the chair.

"I see it," she said in a strangled voice. "I'm inside it. We're nearly here. We just passed into Hexbridge Forest." Her jaw tightened and she stiffened in the chair under the strain. Alfie reached out to take her arm, but Nuala shook her head and he pulled back. He wanted to support her, but couldn't risk breaking her link with the wraith.

"There, there's someone with us," said Amy. "Our master. He wants to be here for the end."

"Can you see his face?" asked Nuala.

Amy shook her head. "I'm trying, but all I can see is a shadow."

"You can do it," whispered Nuala. "Look hard. Tell me what you see."

Amy groaned as she gritted her teeth. "It's a man," she gasped. "He's hooded, I can't see him, but I can feel ... hate. Such hate. He sees me!" She slumped forward in the chair. Madeleine rushed to wrap her arms around Amy's shoulders as Alfie brushed her hair back to see her pale face.

"I'm OK," she said weakly, raising her head. "It was like he knew I was there. He pushed me out before I could see him."

"You did well," said Nuala, handing her another cup of the herbal potion. Amy gulped it down gratefully and Alfie saw some of the fire return to her eyes.

"It's moving fast," said the witch. "We have barely an hour before it reaches the castle. Less time than I thought. I believe I know who travels with it."

"Agrodonn. It's him, isn't it?" said Alfie. "He's coming for me."

"Agrodonn," laughed the witch. "His real name is Baul, but he took a name of destruction from the old books in order to spread fear. A foolish ploy by a foolish man. But foolish men are often the most dangerous. They don't understand the enormity of their actions. In dragging those souls from their grave he has cast a stain on his own that can never be wiped clean. Orin might have taken much of his power from him, but he has had years to learn new tricks. We have a battle coming. Let's be ready for it."

They each took another cup of the strengthening potion. Alfie felt flames burning fiercely in his chest as they stepped out into the courtyard. Robin and Madeleine had grabbed their bows and arrows and Amy had armed herself with a flaming torch, and a shield from the suits of armour in the hall. Alfie had no weapons, but the determination in the eyes of his friends and cousins felt like the strongest of armour. If he had any chance of beating the wraith, it was here, in this place, with them by his side.

The sky was dark, but the beacons on the towers and castle walls lit the courtyard like an arena ready for battle.

Nuala took a stone and scored a wide circle on the cobbles around the oak tree, then nodded to Robin as everyone stepped inside it. Alfie watched as his cousin began to chant the same spell of protection he had cast on the boat and cave. The gold web that shimmered in the air on completion of the spell seemed much stronger now after the strengthening potion. Alfie could see traces of the spell in the air around them, like a golden shield.

"It won't hold for ever, but it will buy you some time," said Robin. "You can do it; we'll be here with you."

"Thanks, Robin," said Alfie, the flame in his chest burning a little stronger.

Madeleine had shimmied up the oak tree and was perched on a sturdy branch, quiver strapped to her back and bow at the ready. Amy was practising thrusts with the torch, as though it were a sword. Nuala had thrown off her cloak and rolled back the sleeves of her dress, ready to work her spells against whatever came into the courtyard. The chickens had made themselves scarce and the sleeping Betsy and Wesley were firmly locked in the stables. The drawbridge was down. There had been no point in raising it for a creature that could pass straight through it.

Alfie tried to stop himself pacing inside the circle as they waited. He had to remember to breathe and stay calm, just as Orin had taught him. *But you're not like Orin,* said that little voice of self-doubt inside him. *You'll never be like him, no matter how hard you try. You're not good enough.* Alfie fought to shut it down before it stole his courage. "Shut up!" he half shouted. No one heard as he was drowned out by a loud howl that carried from the forest up to the castle. It was joined by another, closer, then another closer still. Soon the air was filled with the eerie chorus.

"I sent my friends, the wolves, to warn us of the wraith's approach," said Nuala. "Ready yourselves to fight. It is here."

16

The Unravelling

The howls of the wolves faded away on the still night air. Alfie held his breath in the seemingly infinite silence that followed. The castle's beacons flickered, casting long shadows across the courtyard as the wraith glided over the drawbridge.

"Ready?" Nuala asked.

Alfie nodded, keeping his eyes fixed on the wraith and trying to ignore the chills that crawled over his skin as it drifted closer. It stopped feet away from Alfie as it reached the edge of a protected circle, encased by Nuala and Robin's spells. Raising its hand the wraith reached out towards him. Alfie moved to step back, but the protection held; its hand couldn't pass through, dissolving instead into a smoke-like substance.

"Now, Alfie!" said the witch. Alfie reached down inside himself to his ancient magic. It was already awake and alert, sensing an opportunity to feed. Guiding it towards the talisman on his chest, Alfie focussed on the wraith as it floated before him, sending out little black tendrils to swirl around, searching for a way through the protective dome.

"It won't hold for long, Alfie," said Robin as the web flickered against the night sky. "If you're going to do something, you need to do it now."

Alfie took a deep breath and released it slowly, letting the magic sense the life inside the wraith, the life the creature had taken. Instead of reaching out with his hands as he had with the flames, he reached out through the talisman itself, its lens concentrating the pull of the magic as it latched on to the stolen life-force and began to draw it inside itself, inside Alfie. For a brief second the many voices of the wraith exalted as it felt the touch of the magic it had sought – the voices turned to whispering screams as it felt the life being drawn from it.

Alfie jolted as he felt the wraith begin to fight back, trying to draw the life back into itself along with the magic. He stayed focussed as the wraith morphed into terrifying shapes, twisting demonic shadows, as it fought against him. Alfie ignored its attempts to frighten him, focussing solely on what lay at the heart of the creature, the life it had stolen. He felt as though he was locked in a dangerous tug of war as he ran to follow it in its flight around the circle, fighting for the lives of his friends. It was working; he could feel his magic draining the wraith. It was weakening, its voices becoming cold and fearful.

"Good! Keep going, Alfie!" cried the witch. "Only when you have weakened it by taking back the life it stole can I unbind it from its master's will."

"How sad that you won't be around to live up to that promise," said a chilling voice. From the corner of his eye Alfie saw a man striding into the courtyard. He was dressed all in black, his grey hair drawn back from a pale angular face in which steely eyes glittered malevolently.

"That's him," said Amy. "The man I saw travelling with the wraith."

Alfie's heart seemed to stop for a second as he finally laid eyes on the man responsible for everything that had happened to him over the last year. The one who had brought so much death and destruction to Orin's lands in his search for the magic that Alfie now harboured. Agrodonn.

"Baul!" roared Nuala. "You dare to come back? To challenge Orin, again?"

"It's Agrodonn," the man hissed before raising his hands and looking about the courtyard with a smirk. "And I don't see Orin here. Only an exiled witch and a handful of children." He pointed directly at Alfie. "One of whom holds something that belongs to *me*!" Raising his hands he shot out something like a pulse of energy that sent straw scudding across the courtyard as the web of Robin's protective spell flickered and disappeared in a golden shimmer. Nuala leapt towards Agrodonn, her arms and fingers weaving trails through the air as she repelled the pulses of energy he tried to send towards them.

The wraith took advantage of Alfie's faltering concentration and surged through the broken circle, reaching out towards him. Alfie tripped and fell back on to the cobbles as the terrible sensation of the wraith's touch flooded back into his mind, paralysing him.

"Back!" screamed a voice. Amy had leapt between Alfie and the wraith, waving her flaming torch, stabbing and jabbing at the wraith with it. Robin began to chant in an effort to create a barrier between Amy and the wraith as it swirled away from the flames.

Alfie clambered to his feet and focussed once more on the wraith. It barely had any recognizable form now as it struggled to get past the flames and the small shield of protection Robin had created in front of them. It was like a cloud of angry bees, pulsing and buzzing in the air.

"Hold it there!" shouted Alfie as he reached out again with his magic in an attempt to drain the last of the life energy it held at its heart. He could feel its fear as it fought back against him, clinging on to the precious life it had harvested, but it was greatly weakened now. Alfie exhaled sharply as the last of the stolen lives were drawn into him. The magic was seething with excitement in his chest. Little ripples of energy ran down Alfie's arm to create sparks under his fingernails.

The wraith was letting out a keening noise as it reached out towards them, trying to claw back some of the life it desperately wanted. Robin and Amy were only just managing to hold it back.

Madeleine lit one of her wadded arrows and sent it sailing through the creature – it simply passed through and extinguished on the other side, but it stopped the wraith advancing. "What now?" she called as she lit another.

Alfie looked to Nuala; she was fighting back fiercely against Agrodonn, who was using his powers to tear up cobbles and hurl them towards her as she shattered them in the air. She smashed a small vial at his feet, sending a choking cloud of green smoke rising around the druid, which he dissipated with a blast from his palms. Amy held up her shield just in time for one of the flying cobbles to ricochet off it. "Can you contain the wraith?" Alfie asked Robin. "Like Nuala did down on the beach."

Robin shook his head as he strained to maintain the shield between them and the wraith. "This is the only spell I've mastered. If I try another I won't be able to hold this one. That thing will get through before I can stop it."

Alfie thought fast as Madeleine sent more flaming arrows through the wraith to drive it back. Was there a way they could free it from Agrodonn's will? If only Orin had found a way before it had taken him. The magic welled up inside Alfie, itching to be used. Alfie clenched his fists as he fought against that feeling. He knew he could use the powerful life energy he had drawn from the wraith against it, perhaps even to drive Agrodonn from the castle and save Amy and his cousins, but that would mean burning through the life force of Orin and the others to save himself.

"Orin!" Alfie cried out as a realization hit him. Nuala had told him that he could save Orin and Bryn by facing the wraith; maybe he had everything he needed to do that now.

"Keep holding it back!" he yelled to the others as he ran for the castle door. The wraith made a move to follow but Robin pushed it back like a lion tamer with a chair as Madeleine and Amy kept it at bay with fire.

"Where are you going?" Amy yelled.

"To get help!"

Alfie skidded into the Great Hall and over to Orin.

"OK, what now?" he whispered to himself as he looked down at the druid's still body. He had taken back Orin's life, but how was he supposed to return it to the druid? The wraith had drained the life from around a dozen people, as well as from Wesley the goat and Bryn's horse, and now it was all mixed together inside Alfie. What if he gave Wesley's life to the druid? Would it matter? And what if he gave too much, or too little? He wished the witch was there to advise him, but if he didn't do this now, there might not be anyone left alive to advise him.

He remembered Orin saying something about taking with the left hand and giving with the right while he had practised with the magic. Taking his right hand, he placed it on Orin's chest. At that point he didn't even need to think about what to do – he could feel Orin's life force flare up within him and begin to flow back into the druid's body, making its way home.

The ancient magic roared inside Alfie as it realized he was giving away the strongest energy it had harvested. It tried to hold on to its prize, but Alfie beat it back down, forcing it into submission as he returned the druid's life force. As the last of Orin's life returned home, Alfie waited – jaw clenched, hardly daring to breathe. After what seemed like an age the druid's eyelids flickered and he drew a long wheezing breath.

Alfie ran to grab a cup from the table and filled it with the strengthening potion. Putting his arm under Orin's shoulders, he lifted him to a sitting position and brought the cup to his lips. The liquid spilled out down Orin's beard, but as it moistened his lips the druid began to drink. The crashing of falling masonry echoed in from the courtyard along with the shouts and yells of the twins and Amy as they fought to keep the wraith at bay.

"Come on, Orin," Alfie whispered. "We need you!"

The cup fell to the floor as the druid drained the last drops and looked up at Alfie. The lifeless stare was gone from his eyes, Orin was back.

"Alfie!" he cried, grasping his arm and pulling himself to his feet. He looked to Bryn, and Ashford laid out next to him. "Tell me, what has happened since the wraith found me?"

"We got your message," said Alfie, as Orin staggered over to draw himself another draught of the potion. "We brought back Nuala. The wraith got Bryn on our way to find her. It's here now, and so is Agrodonn. Nuala is fighting him, and Amy and the twins are holding off the wraith. You've got to help us!"

Orin drained the cup, wiped his mouth with the back of his hand and drew himself up to his full height. His grey eyes flashed with anger. "This ends now!" He slammed the cup on to the table and charged through the castle out into the courtyard, robes billowing behind him. Alfie sprinted after him, astounded at the druid's quick recovery.

Madeleine, Amy and Robin were standing back to back, holding off the wraith with everything they had. It was clear they were tiring and the wraith had gathered itself together and was reaching out for them with its long tendril fingers.

"Agrodonn!" roared Orin as he saw him ducking and weaving around the courtyard with Nuala as they dodged and parried each other's spells. "You dare to return here?" He leapt to take Nuala's place, robes whirling as he raised his hands and swept aside one of Agrodonn's spells, obliterating a stone planter.

Nuala ducked and rolled over to the twins and Amy just as Madeleine fired her last flaming arrow and Robin sank to the ground in exhaustion. As Amy stood over them waving her torch, Nuala began to cast a binding spell, trapping the swirling wraith once more inside a bubble.

Alfie was worried about Orin; it soon became clear that he was nowhere near his full strength and was only just holding his own against the other druid.

"You are weak," shouted Agrodonn, pushing forwards. "Since last we met I have been rebuilding my strength, and biding my time. Now the magic you hid from me is right here inside this boy. All you have to do to save yourselves is to give it to me."

"Never," shouted Orin.

Alfie noticed that Orin was only deflecting Agrodonn's spells and wasn't firing back his own. Was it because he was weakened, or because he didn't want to cause harm?

"And you, boy! Would you risk your friends for the sake of holding on to a magic that you don't want?"

"I'd be risking their lives just as much if I gave it to you," shouted Alfie, pushing down the magic that was itching to be let loose with the energy it had absorbed.

Agrodonn roared in anger and sent a flaming bolt into the oak tree, splitting a large branch from its trunk.

"Look out!" screamed Alfie as he tumbled towards his cousins. Amy dropped her torch and dragged Madeleine out of the way. Robin was a second too slow and disappeared under the leaves before Nuala could pull him to safety.

"No! You will not harm anyone else!" shouted Orin, sending a whirling gust of wind straight at

Agrodonn, which unbalanced the druid and caused him to stagger back.

"That's more like it," grinned Agrodonn. "Let's fight for the magic while the home you built with it burns around us." He sent a burst of flame over his shoulder towards the stables as he advanced on Orin, easily deflecting the weakened druid's counter-spells.

Alfie stared in horror as flames engulfed the stable where Betsy, Wesley and Orin's horse lay. He looked to Nuala but she was working to both hold the wraith and move the branch that had landed on Robin, as Madeleine and Amy struggled to pull him free. Rushing to the stable as the flames licked at the straw roof, Alfie focussed on drawing the ferocious energy of the flames into himself. Using the magic was getting easier each time and the flames died down quickly as their power flowed into him. Alfie couldn't bear the sensation as the magic feasted again. Its whispers were now roaring inside his head. He had to use it, had to get rid of the energy he had just taken from the flames.

There was a sudden cry of triumph. Alfie whirled around to see Orin thrown to the ground as Agrodonn advanced on him. Orin didn't get up;

he lay rigid on the cobbles, stunned by the spell that had hit him. Alfie had to do something. As Agrodonn leaned over Orin ready to deliver a final spell, Alfie let his magic loose with the energy it had just feasted on. Summoning a ball of flame to his hand, he hurled it at the cackling druid.

Agrodonn shrieked as it hit him. Tearing his flaming cloak from his shoulders, he threw it to the ground. He looked and Alfie was sure he saw a hint of fear in his wild eyes, but his sneer returned as he saw Alfie hesitate in using the magic again.

"Hah! You think having magic makes you like *us*?" he spat.

"Us? You're nothing like him," said Alfie, nodding towards Orin. "He'd *never* hurt anyone for his own gain."

"Really?" laughed Agrodonn, waving his arm at Amy, Madeleine and Nuala, who were still frantically trying to free Robin. "Plenty of people have been hurt because of Orin, all because he was too selfish to give up a magic that he didn't even need. Think of the life you could be living now without that magic inside you, whispering to you, weighing you down. I could take it from you, save you from it, leave you all to live your lives in peace."

"As if I could live in peace, knowing I'd given a weapon like that to someone like you," said Alfie, trying hard to hold his ground as Agrodonn advanced towards him.

"Very well," hissed the druid. "You had your chance." Raising his hands, he shrieked out a spell and hurled two balls of flame towards Alfie. But Alfie was ready, creating a blast of icy wind that extinguished the flames and blew Agrodonn back a few paces. The druid snarled and thrust out his hands, sending out blasts of energy that tore up the cobbles to fly towards Alfie. Alfie created flaming bolts of his own to shatter the cobbles in the air, then ducked and rolled to avoid the ones he couldn't catch as they whizzed by him.

Nuala called to him, but the wraith was beginning to tear itself free from its prison and she had to fight to contain it. With her free arm she gestured wildly at the shield Amy had dropped.

A shield! He needed to make a shield. If only he could perform Orin's protection spell, just like Robin. Then it dawned on him: maybe he could, in a different way! Alfie focussed on letting the magic flow through the talisman, forming an invisible barrier between himself and the druid. It worked. The cobbles pummelled the shield between them.

It held fast, but Alfie felt himself being pushed backwards with each blow. He groaned with the effort of maintaining the barrier as Agrodonn hurled spells and stones at it with all his might.

As Alfie staggered back under the raining blows he felt water seeping through his boots. He glanced down, realizing he had stepped back into the pond in the courtyard garden. The split second of lost concentration was enough. Agrodonn launched his most powerful attack yet – the force sent Alfie skidding backwards, his feet slid out from under him on the slimy bed of the pond. The shield evaporated as he toppled back into the water, muddy water flowing into his nose and mouth.

Agrodonn didn't waste a second. By the time Alfie surfaced, coughing water from his lungs, the druid was upon him. Two powerful hands gripped his tunic. Alfie splashed around trying to fight back, but was thrust firmly below the water. Alfie held his breath as he tried to tear away from the druid's grasp, but he was too strong. His lungs burned as he fought the urge to take a breath. At last he felt himself being dragged back to the surface, and he gulped down huge gasps of air the second his head left the water. Agrodonn was crouched over him. He dragged Alfie up until his nose was within an inch of his own.

"I want my face to be the last thing you see," he growled, wrapping his hands around Alfie's throat. "When you take your last breath and the magic leaves your body, it will be mine at last."

Alfie thrashed around, unable to scream for help as Agrodonn squeezed his neck. He felt his face flush red as he struggled to breathe, grasping and scratching at the druid's hands. As his lungs screamed for air, Alfie forced the magic back to life, directing it towards the talisman on his chest. The edges of his vision seemed to be going dark. With every scrap of will he could muster he forged the energy he had drawn from the fire into a bright bolt of energy. It surged up from inside him and blasted out through the talisman as a brilliant white light, throwing the druid across the courtyard to crash to the cobbles, limp as a rag doll.

Alfie dragged himself from the pond on his knees and leaned over to rest his forehead on the ground as he coughed the rest of the water from his lungs.

"Alfie!" shouted Amy, grabbing him by the shoulders. "Are you OK?"

Alfie nodded as he flopped back on to the grass.

"Robin?" he gasped.

"We got him out. He's unconscious and I think his leg might be broken, but he's alive."

Alfie leaned heavily on Amy as she pulled him to his feet. The wraith was hovering nearby, bound by Nuala's magic. The witch had run to help Orin. The druid was on his feet now, the effects of the stunning spell having worn off. They were standing over Agrodonn, who lay motionless on the cobbles. The cold hand of fear clenched Alfie's stomach as he staggered over to them.

"Is he ... he's not ... is he?" he asked, unable to bring himself to say the word.

"No Alfie, he's not dead," said Orin.

"But he'll soon wish he was," said Nuala, grabbing his leg and dragging him roughly across the courtyard with a strength that made Amy beam with admiration. The witch muttered a spell and Agrodonn's limp body was thrown against the oak tree and bound there as if with invisible ropes.

"Did he hurt you?" asked Alfie, looking up at Orin.

"More than he could ever have hoped to if I'd been my usual self," said the druid. "But I'll be fine after a long rest, and Nuala's care. Right now, we have bigger problems to deal with." He looked up at the wraith, which was still trying to break out of its prison, tendrils beginning to emerge from weak spots in the bubble that encased it.

Agrodonn was starting to come around and was enraged to find himself bound to the oak. His eyes were full of hate as he glared at Orin and Alfie. He struggled to free himself and Alfie could see his fingers twitching, desperate to hurl spells at them.

"Why did you come back?" asked Orin. "Are you still so angry and hungry for power after our last encounter. After all these years? You could have moved on, accepted your loss and lived a full life making amends for your crimes. But, no. You learnt nothing. You sought out more magic in your quest for power." Orin's voice rose as he pointed at the wraith. Alfie had never seen him look so furious. "You tore these poor souls from their resting place and bent them to your will, letting them take the lives of the innocent, and THEN ... you come back *here*, to my *home*, harm my friends and try once more to take the magic I swore you would never have. *Why?*"

Agrodonn stared defiantly back at him, a smirk playing around his lips.

"Why not?"

Orin said nothing, but the muscles of his jaw were pulled tight. Alfie could see he was fighting to remain in control of himself. Nuala was doing no such thing.

"Release the wraith," she growled, grasping Agrodonn by the throat.

"Make me," he spat.

"Nuala, stop," said Orin as the witch raised her hand in front of her prisoner's face and began to chant. She paused, but did not let go of his throat.

Alfie glanced at the wraith. It had finally broken out of its prison and was beginning to pour out of it in a thin stream, reforming on the other side.

"Orin, it's going to come for us again," said Alfie.

The druid sighed. "Agrodonn, if you will not release it from your curse, we have no choice but to do it for you."

"And you know what that means," added Nuala.

Agrodonn looked from one to the other. "You wouldn't dare," he hissed.

"You leave us no choice," said Orin, grasping Agrodonn's wrist.

"Stop, I'll do it," Agrodonn cried, but Nuala had already pulled a silver knife from her belt and slashed it across his palm. Dark droplets of blood splashed down on to the ground.

The wraith was drifting towards them, its whispers growing louder as it reached out for Alfie. Orin dipped his finger in the blood and began to chant as he traced out a symbol on the ground. Alfie flinched back as the wraith's long fingers reached for his chest, preparing himself for the terrible icy chill – but it didn't come. The wraith had stopped. Its form began to shift until it was no longer a human shape, but a swirling cloud, no longer black but a shimmering silver.

Orin finished his chant and Nuala wet her fingers with Agrodonn's blood and flicked it into the silver cloud. It exploded outwards with a sound like a hundred soft cries of relief. *Were these the individual souls Agrodonn had bound together?* thought Alfie as he stared at the silver wisps.

"Now go," shouted Orin. "Back to your rest."

But the wisps remained, illuminating the courtyard with their gentle light.

"Why aren't they leaving? What do they want?" asked Alfie.

"No," cried Agrodonn, eyes wide with fear. "Don't let them do this! Don't let them take me!"

Orin turned away. From the look on his face Alfie knew that the druid could do nothing to prevent whatever was about to happen.

Agrodonn screamed as the souls flowed towards him. The silver cloud enveloped him, wrenching him from the tree and dragging him across the courtyard.

"Help me," he screamed wildly, grasping at Alfie as he was borne past. His fingers slipped from Alfie's sleeve as the souls carried him away, through the gatehouse, over the drawbridge, down Hexbridge Hill and away into the velvet night. Soon his distant screams faded and all was still once more.

17

Warriors All

"You'd think that having his life force drained would have calmed him down a bit," said Amy, fighting a tug of war with Wesley the goat as he tried to steal her boots for the fourth time. It was a sunny afternoon, and as Alfie lay on the grass in the peaceful courtyard, he could hardly believe anything bad had happened there just days before.

He turned his head to watch Robin walking around the courtyard supported by Madeleine. He was limping a little, but the healing powers of a druid, a witch and his own twin sister had gone a long way to mending Robin's leg with incredible speed. When they returned home in a couple of days there would be no sign he'd ever had a broken bone. It would be gone without a trace – much like Agrodonn. Alfie tried to forget Agrodonn's screams as the released souls had dragged their former master away with them to who knew where, perhaps down into the plague pit from where he had summoned them. Alfie shivered in the warm sun.

The *chop-chop* of Bryn and Ashford splitting logs drifted over from the stables. Alfie had returned the life that the wraith had stolen from them and Nuala and Madeleine's potions had nursed them back to health. They seemed quite recovered from their ordeal, as were the people of Miggleswick who Alfie had visited with Orin and Nuala. They didn't remember much about the wraith's visit, and the druid had convinced them that they had been suffering from a sleeping sickness.

"Best to let them believe a less terrifying reality," Orin had said.

The worst side effect for Bryn was the guilt he seemed to feel over leaving them to make the journey to Demon Rock alone. He had scratched his arm and shifted uncomfortably when they had brought up his transformation into a bear.

"It's a family thing," he had said, looking

at his feet. "My mother, her mother, my great grandfather – they could all transform. I imagine I scared you all pretty badly. I . . . well, I understand if you won't dare have anything to do with me now." He had made as if to stand up. "I'll be off, and I'll be sure to make myself scarce whenever you visit."

He hadn't managed to make it to his feet before Alfie, Amy and the twins had flung themselves on him.

"You're not going anywhere!" Madeleine had yelled, throwing her arms around him.

"Yeah, you saved us back in the forest!" said Robin.

"As if we could be scared of you," added Alfie with a grin. "Back at home our best friend is a bear."

Bryn blinked quickly and swallowed hard. "Well, that's very kind of you lads and lasses," he said gruffly. "Well then, I'll stick around, if you're sure?"

"Sure? We couldn't *bear* to be without you," Amy had said, giving him a squeeze.

"Hah! A word joke!" he had boomed. "I'm always happy to *paws* what I'm doing for one of those!"

Alfie had shaken his head. "Don't get him started on those too. One friend that puns is more than enough."

Something pricked at the back of Alfie's brain as he lay on the grass, remembering that conversation with Bryn. Two friends that pun, both of them bears – was that more than a coincidence?

"Hey, Alfie," said Robin, hobbling over. "I've been working on something for you." Madeleine grabbed her brother's arm and he eased himself on to the grass next to Alfie. "Here." Robin handed over a small package wrapped in cloth.

"What is it?" asked Alfie. At the sound of his voice the package began to bounce in his hands, letting out muffled chirps. "I don't believe it," he said, untying the bindings. The second the wrapping fell open, something rocketed out of it in a silver blur, whizzing round and round their heads before coming to rest on Alfie's shoulder.

"Sparky! You fixed him." Alfie slapped Robin on the back as the silver sparrow nuzzled his ear. "And he's just the same as he was."

"Yeah, an annoying silver idiot," grinned Madeleine.

"Better wrap him back up until we get home," said Robin. "Before he gets himself seen."

"Incoming," said Amy, sitting up. Alfie tucked the protesting bird back into its wrappings and followed Amy's gaze up into the sky. A large raven was swooping purposefully down towards them.

"Caspian," said Alfie, getting to his feet as the raven began to morph into a man as its talons hit the ground. Feathers became an immaculately tailored Victorian-style black suit, wings folded and became arms as the solicitor reached out to shake hands with Alfie, then Amy and the twins.

"Long time, no see," said Amy without a trace of a smile.

"You are well?" asked Caspian.

"We are now," said Alfie stiffly, jaw clenched at such a simple question after everything that had happened over the last week.

"No thanks to you lot," said Amy. Alfie was always amazed at how she dared to speak to Caspian like that. Alfie was still angry at Mr Muninn's response to their plea for help, but too wary of Caspian's sharp tongue to express that anger.

"I. . ." Caspian swallowed before continuing as though having difficulty with an unfamiliar word. "I am *sorry* that Mr Muninn did not extend our help to you during my absence."

293

Alfie stared at Caspian, wide-eyed. An apology, whatever next? He wondered about Caspian's relationship with Mr Muninn. Alfie had only met him that once in his raven form, but from Emily Fortune, the firm's senior administrator, he had gathered that Mr Muninn made Caspian seem jolly in comparison.

"It's fine for you to say that, but couldn't you just have gone back in time to help us? You're here in the past now!" said Amy. The slight softness Alfie had heard in Caspian's voice disappeared.

"Our offices exist outside of time – you could never hope to understand the complexities of that. While I am sorry that you have experienced a great deal, I cannot, and will not, attempt to change what has occurred here. Now, you will excuse me while I speak with Orin."

Alfie left Amy glowering and hurried after the solicitor, catching him in the doorway to the castle.

"Caspian. May I ask you something?"

The solicitor looked down at him. "You may ask anything you wish. Whether you get an answer is at my discretion."

"Artan," said Alfie, searching Caspian's eyes for a reaction. "You told me not to bring him because he doesn't exist here yet. I'm thinking, maybe he does exist here, but not as we know him." He glanced pointedly at Bryn who was still merrily chopping logs.

Caspian paused for a few seconds and Alfie knew that his terrible suspicion was true. Bryn *was* Artan. He had been killed while in his bear form. Alfie thought frantically – could he warn Bryn? Would that save him from his terrible fate?

"You are wondering if you can save him?" asked Caspian. "Even if you could warn him of the exact moment of his death, it is likely that it would happen in another way. And if you were to change his destiny, what of the times Artan has saved you? Would any of you be here now if not for his help?"

Alfie bit his lip hard and hugged his stomach to try and stop the ache there. Artan seemed happy as a flying bearskin, but surely he would prefer to lead an ordinary life and die as an old man? But would Alfie's family and friends still be alive if Artan hadn't saved him so many times?

"Act as you see fit," said Caspian. "But be aware that your life as it stands is the best it could be. Tamper with time at the risk of all you hold dear." At this he left Alfie standing alone in the cool entrance hall as he climbed the stairs and headed to Orin's study.

Alfie thought long and hard on Caspian's words over the next couple of days while Bryn laughed and joked with them and shared the tricks and knowledge of a medieval woodsman. His heart was heavy in his chest as Bryn said goodbye on the afternoon they were to travel home. He couldn't warn him; he couldn't risk the alternative to the future as it stood.

Bryn reached out to shake his hand, but Alfie pushed it away and hugged him tightly, hiding his face in Bryn's thick sheepskin waistcoat.

"Be careful, OK?" he said when he felt it was safe to show his face again. "You know, when you're out and about."

"I always am, lad, always am," said Bryn with a smile. His happy whistle as he strode away down Hexbridge Hill made Alfie's heart sink lower still.

Nuala had stayed at the castle with the excuse of brewing strengthening potions for all affected by the wraith, but Amy had been quick to point out that there seemed more to it than that.

"All I'm saying is that they seem to be *very* good friends," she had said the previous night, a sly grin playing on her lips as the druid and the witch went for a night walk down to the forest to collect herbs by moonlight.

"It was an honour to meet you," said Nuala as they gathered in the courtyard, ready to make the journey home. "May the protection of the sea go with you," she said to each of them as she tied bracelets made of tiny shells around their wrists. They were braided together with slightly seaweedy rope that Alfie suspected had come from one of the wrecks out by her island.

"Thank you. For all of your help," said Alfie as she finished tying his to his wrist.

"You hardly needed it," she smiled. "You have great strength inside you, Alfie, and I'm not talking about the magic you guard. You need to recognize your own worth."

Alfie gritted his teeth a little at this, wishing he had as much confidence in himself as everyone else seemed to have in him. Why did they all seem to think that they knew him better than he knew himself?

"I am sorry that your training did not proceed quite the way we had planned," said Orin as they all crossed the courtyard to sit down near the gargoyle fountain. "But it seems you learnt much without my tuition. Rest, for now. Your training will begin again once you have recovered from what happened here."

Alfie picked at his fingernails as he looked down at his feet.

"Have I said something to upset you, Alfie?" asked the druid gently.

Alfie sighed, knowing that what he was about to say could send him back to the scruffy flat where he had lived with his dad only a year ago, although it seemed like a decade now, but he couldn't not tell Orin the truth.

"I can't do this," he said quietly. "I can't be a druid. I'm nothing like you. You've given me all these books about magic, but I can't understand them. Not at all. Robin can read the runes and recite the spells – he protected us all so many times and I can't even understand a single page!" Once he had started to speak Alfie felt the words well up in an unstoppable flow. "Madeleine can mix potions and ointments better than any modern medicine, but I wouldn't know where to start – or how she tells the difference between all the plants! And now Amy! She can somehow see things that are happening elsewhere. We'd all have been drained by the wraith, and Agrodonn would have the magic from inside me if Amy hadn't warned us the wraith was coming when we were in the barn. I can't do spells, I can't brew potions, I don't have any special skills! All I can do is barely hold on to the magic you gave me to protect. Why would you want me to be your apprentice? I can't learn everything you have to teach me. Maybe you should take on someone else – someone better than me. Pass your knowledge on to one of them." He waved his hand towards the twins and Amy then stared at the grass, breathing deeply, embarrassed but relieved that he had unloaded all that had been bothering him so deeply. Would Orin be furious? Would he leave the castle to someone else? Someone worthy of it?

Everyone was quiet, waiting for the druid to speak. Alfie felt his muscles trembling, but was glad that he had finally said everything he had been holding in for so long.

"Someone better than you?" said Orin at last. "Alfie, you have within you a magic that could be harnessed to do great and terrible things. When it was mine it would whisper to me, begging me to let it feed and use it to create my heart's desires. Do you realize the strength it takes to refuse that call? To keep it from corrupting you?" Alfie looked up to meet Orin's grey eyes as he realized there was no anger in the druid's voice. "My dear friend, that immense strength is your gift. The strength to guard and hold back a magic that could cause great chaos should it be used for selfish wants."

Alfie had always assumed that Orin had no trouble with the magic when it was his, but it had whispered to the druid too. Orin knew exactly how he felt when the magic hungered to feed and be used. Suddenly Alfie didn't feel so alone in his internal struggles, but his fears about becoming Orin's apprentice remained.

"Even if that's my gift, it doesn't help me learn everything you want to teach me. It's too much, I just can't do it."

"Whoever said you had to do this alone?" the druid smiled. "Look about you, know your loved ones." He touched the twins and Amy on their shoulders one by one. "Madeleine – the Healer. Robin – the Scholar. Amy – the Seer." Finally he placed his hand on Alfie's own shoulder. "And you – the Guardian, warriors all. Between you I have a greater apprentice than any druid could ever hope for."

Alfie looked to Amy and the twins, they all beamed back at him.

"Are you sure?" he asked them. "You really want to do this with me?"

"Seriously?" said Amy, shaking her head. "We've

been with you all along. It's not like we're going to stop now."

Alfie's heart soared. All this time he had kept his fears locked up inside, yet all along he had everything he needed in his cousins and best friend. A warmth, stronger than any strengthening potion could create, burned strongly inside him as he bade goodbye to Orin and Nuala, joined hands with the twins and Amy and let himself flow back through time, pulled forward to where they belonged. Home.

After catching up with his dad – after the twins and Amy went home – after the castle's lights were turned down low – and after Galileo had curled up by his feet, Alfie slipped out of bed and climbed the spiral staircase to Artan's tower room. The bear somersaulted through the air in delight to see him.

"Fancy a quick flight?" asked Alfie.

The treetops whizzed by below them as Artan dipped and soared on their flight over hills and forests. After sharing the story of what had happened in the past and groaning over at least a dozen terrible puns the bear had thought up in his absence, Alfie went quiet. Artan didn't interrupt the silence as they flew out over the North Sea. Alfie gazed down at a group of islands below them, spotting Demon Rock by the rocky pillars that still jutted out from the sea around it. He could barely believe that they had sailed out there in a fierce storm six hundred years ago, though really only a week ago. The witch's hut was long gone. He wondered what had happened to Nuala. Had she returned to the island and lived out the rest of her life there, diving with her fellow seals and talking to the birds?

"Artan," began Alfie, finally daring to ask the questions that had been hovering on his lips since leaving the castle. "When we first met, you told us you didn't remember much about your life before you became a rug. How much *do* you remember?"

"This and that," said the bear after a pause. "Memories come and go when you're hundreds of years old. I don't see the need to cling to them."

"But you *do* remember that we've had adventures together before. You told us that after our first flight. The adventure we've just had, the journey to Demon Rock to save Orin, did any of that sound familiar to you – as if you were there?"

Artan was silent for longer this time. Alfie hated pushing him, but he had to know.

"There's little to be had from looking backwards," said the bear at last. "The future is always so much more interesting."

Alfie knew then that the bear did have some memories of his previous existence, his life as Bryn the woodsman. He just had one more question to ask.

"Are you happy? I mean, if you had a choice, if your life could have been different, if I could do something about it – would you want that?"

Artan rippled slightly in the breeze then swooped down to skim the water so that the gentle sea spray caught their faces, then soared up over the islands as the seals barked at them.

"What time is there to be unhappy?" asked Artan, his fur damp and windswept, eyes bright. "I have all I want, and all I need. Who is to say what would have been? But I don't regret a minute of the life I've lived. I have the greatest of companions, and adventures still waiting to be had. Here and now, I am happy and wouldn't change a thing."

Unable to find words Alfie hugged the bear tightly around his shaggy neck. Artan did a little flip and turned back towards Hexbridge. Rolling on to his back, Alfie breathed a happy sigh. He felt grateful for his companions too. No longer would he feel inadequate, unable to fulfil his destiny. He didn't have to do anything alone. Gazing up into the star spattered sky he repeated Orin's words,

The Healer, the Scholar, the Seer, the Guardian – warriors all.

ACKNOWLEDGEMENTS

Last summer my husband and I paid a visit to the Poison Garden within Alnwick Gardens. I would like to thank our guide, Len Reece, for giving us such a great overview of toxic plants and how some of them were used in medieval times. A couple of those grisly anecdotes informed parts of this book, and the others will continue to cause us nightmares.

I would also like to take this opportunity to say thank you to librarians everywhere. Without you many writers may never have discovered a love of books and gone on to write their own, and many children may never have discovered our stories. From my Saturday morning visits to Hartlepool library with my dad, through afternoons in the school library where I would practise my writing skills, to days working on the Alfie Bloom series in many libraries across the North of England, every minute has helped me on my journey as a writer.

Librarians continue to help me by inviting me to speak at events, organizing my book launches, nominating my books for awards, and sharing my work with young people, some of whom don't have access to books at home. Every time I visit a library I see something new that you, our librarians, are doing to bring our communities together. It saddens me that libraries are closing because the people who hold the purse strings cannot see the enormity of what you actually do. But know this, to the rest of us you are heroes.

Have you read all of Alfie's adventures in
Hexbridge Castle?

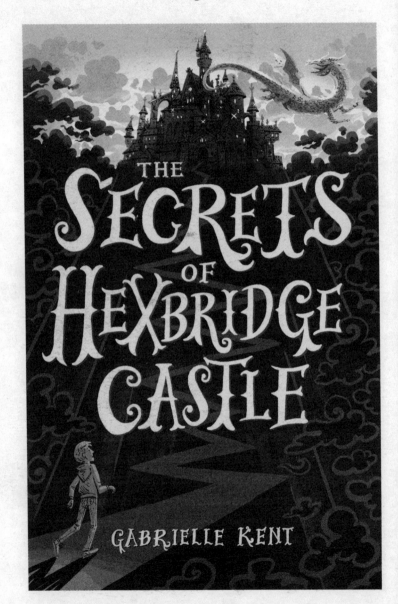

THE TALISMAN THIEF

GABRIELLE KENT

Gabrielle Kent has worked in and around the games industry since 1997 and currently lectures in Computer Games Development at Teesside University. As well as teaching, she directs Animex, the UK's largest Games and Animation Festival. In 2015 she received games magazine MCV's Woman of the Year Award. She loves writing just as much as games and dreams of one day writing books in the library of her very own castle.

gabriellekent.com
@GabrielleKent